D0891694

WINTER STORIES

INGVILD H. RISHØI

WINTER STORIES

Translated by Diane Oatley

LONDON NEW YORK CALCUTTA

This translation has been published with
the financial support of NORLA

Seagull Books, 2019

Originally published as Ingvild H. Rishøi, *Vinternoveller*
© Gyldendal Norsk Forlag AS, 2014. All rights reserved.

First published in English translation by Seagull Books, 2019

English translation © Diane Oatley, 2019

ISBN   978 0 8574 2 610 9

British Library Cataloguing-in-Publication Data
A catalogue record for this book is available from the British
Library

Typeset by Seagull Books, Calcutta, India
Printed and bound by WordsWorth India, New Delhi, India

CONTENTS

WE CAN'T HELP EVERYBODY

Alexa wets herself when we reach Linderud. We were going to walk all the way home, she was with me on that, there's no point in spending money on bus fare for only five stops. But now we've just made it past the shopping centre, we haven't even made it halfway.

I did ask her if it was fine if we walked. And she climbed up on the gate to the kindergarten and opened the chain latch and said *yes, Mummy*.

She says nothing now, but she starts walking with her legs spread apart and I know she's cold. Because it's December. The sky is dark. Her reflector dangles below the hem of her jacket.

60 minus 45 equals 15. 15 kroner left.

But I can't dodge the bus fare, not with her, because she notices everything I do, she watches me all the time, and if we board the bus from the door in the back, she will stop in front of the ticket machine and say: 'Do we have tickets, Mummy?'

And the buildings twinkle, and Alexa rocks from side to side, and the cars roar, and the lamp posts are covered with graffiti lettering, I remember Alex wrote my name like that, behind the gymnasium, and I don't say anything about her wetting herself, but I know that when we get home, she'll rush into the bathroom and close the door and in a few days I'll find her panties, crumpled up, at the bottom of the linen hamper, that's how she is, that's how it goes, that's how she is.

But I can't bear to watch her rocking like that.

'Let's take the bus,' I say.

She looks up.

'Yes,' she says. 'Maybe that would be better.'

We turn around. The shopping centre glitters. They have decorated it with strings of criss-crossing lights, it's supposed to look like a present.

Then Alexa takes my hand and stops.

There's a boy standing in front of us. He smiles, we are maybe the same age. He's good-looking. He's holding a paper cup in his hand.

'Could you help me out with some change?' he says.

His fingers are swollen. Alexa squeezes my hand. She feels so sorry for everyone, far too sorry, like that daft business with her dolls, when she gets completely obsessed about making sure the duvet is drawn up to their chins, they lie there at the foot of her bed and she sits up twenty times every night to make sure that it's fair. She must change. She must become more like me.

'Sorry,' I say, and start walking.

The hems of his sweatpants are filthy and I can see Alexa's legs, her movements are so awkward and stiff. That's how it goes. That's how it goes, I remember all those girls, with an 'x' in their calendars and morning-after pills in their wallets, that's how it goes when you're not like them. There's the bus stop. We probably have something in the freezer, we'll just have to manage, she can't walk home like that.

Now she looks up.

'Mummy,' she says. 'Why?'

'Why what?' I say.

She has this tendency to think that I am inside her head.

We stand and wait at the bus stop. I look towards the bend in the road, no bus coming there.

INGVILD H. RISHØI

Now her wet panties must be freezing against her skin.

'Why not?' she says.

Oh, it irritates me. We are two people, she must simply just accept it.

'But you have to say a bit more when I don't understand what you mean,' I say. 'You have to explain a bit better.'

'Why couldn't we help him out with some change?' she says.

I look towards the bend in the road again.

Because there is no such thing as small change. Because your father hasn't paid child support in three months, didn't you notice that he didn't call on your birthday, I put you to bed with your birthday crown from kindergarten on your head, and afterwards I sat at the kitchen table with my feet up on the chair and my forehead on my knees, he's thinking about other girls now, do you see these two 10-kroner coins and these two 20-kroner coins? They have to get us through the rest of the weekend. Do you see this tattoo, it's your father's name and if I could afford it, I would have it changed into a bird, I have even drawn that bird, on greaseproof paper, one evening I sat at the kitchen table, and the bird

4

turned out nicely, the wings lifting at the tips, it looked like it was taking flight.

It starts to rain. I pull up the hood on her jacket.

'We can't help everybody,' I say.

Because when Alexa looks at me, she sees an adult. And when Alex picks her up, she sees an adult, he holds the basketball in one hand and her hand with the other, then they disappear down the road, she thinks he's an adult, but he doesn't know anything about adult things, he never puts on the blue shoe covers in the kindergarten, he doesn't know what a maturity date is or what to do with a child who wets herself all the time, he couldn't be bothered one bit about those stickers she was supposed to win if she could hold it, even though at the health clinic they said that we had to be consistent.

The only thing he knows how to do is play basketball.

And the only thing she sees is Daddy, Daddy, Daddy. And as for me, the only thing that I remember is his hands all over me and how he moved when he was preparing to jump. He hung in the air for so long. And when she was born, I remember what he said. He bent down over the bed and said: 'She looks just like me. She looks exactly the hell like me. We must call her Alexa.'

It's the truth.

I see it all the time. In how she runs, in how she moves her body.

And all of a sudden she closes her eyes and clenches her fists, with her arms straight down, like a penguin.

'But he didn't have a hand!' she says. 'Didn't you see?'

She shakes her head. Now she's falling apart in the way that she does.

'He didn't have a hand?' I say.

'Just one,' she says. 'Don't you notice anything, Mummy?'

I squat down. Her knapsack slides down off my shoulder. Her head sways from side to side.

'Alexa,' I say.

But I don't know what else I can say. The cars keep coming and coming and coming. I never have anything really wise to say, I didn't have anything before and nothing more was forthcoming after I had a baby. I lean against her. The rain patters on her hood.

That sound. It reminds me of the caravan.

The raindrops on the roof.

And Mum when she was happy, when the sky cleared and she sat in the opening of the tent with her eyes closed and her face towards the sun. *If you trample moss for the third time, it will never spring back up again*, Mum said. *The third time you go under, you drown.*

She lit the mosquito coil and a cigarette. She exhaled smoke and squinted at the ocean.

Now everything is so different. One thing after another has changed, and now I have a job and a daughter and days like this, and here I sit on the pavement and she is five years old and shakes her head, and squeezes her eyes shut, but the sound of the rain creates something light inside of me.

That everything can be different again.

Everything can be fine.

I look around.

There he is, standing under a street lamp. It may well be that he just has one hand. She's probably right, she tends to notice everything, who is working the late shift on what day, how many eggs are left in the refrigerator, for sure he has only one hand.

I get to my feet and wrap my hand around her fist. She needs rain mittens, they cost maybe 100 kroner, and her hands are so wet and cold. Then I say: 'We'll have to go back then. He's still standing there.'

She opens her eyes then. She leans back her head. Her hood slides off. And that face of hers, it's shining, she is so pretty, she always has been, I remember when they bathed her at the hospital and Alex turned to the nurses and said: *Look at that mouth, have you ever seen such a baby before? She's going to be just as beautiful as her mother.*

'Are we going to help him out?' Alexa says.

'Yes,' I say. 'I didn't know that he only had one hand.'

Then she starts to hop. First straight up and down, and then forward, her reflector blinks, she bounces and I lead her, on the pavement, between all the people, and my arm tilts up and down as she hops.

He is wearing a hooded sweatshirt. He smiles.

'I have some small change after all,' I say.

I find my wallet and unzip the coin pocket. A siren begins to howl behind us, Alexa puts her hands over her ears, then the siren stops howling and Alexa drops her hands and I release the coin.

And then I see what kind of coin it is. But it's too late.

It's a 20-kroner coin.

I was going to give him a tenner.

But it's too late now.

I gave away 20 kroner.

There it is, at the bottom of his paper cup. Now we can't take the bus, she'll have to walk home in wet panties, but she doesn't know that, so she's just smiling and he winks at her and says:

'Thank you very much.'

But the pee won't dry in this weather and if she gets a bladder infection, I'll have to call Alex's mother, I can't stay home from work any more now, I've had twenty sick days, I lose 800 kroner a day if I stay at home.

'You're welcome,' Alexa says.

'What a pretty daughter you have,' he says.

'Thanks,' I say.

But what am I supposed to do now?

If only we could dodge the bus fare. But she can't handle it, I don't understand why, I'm not the one who explained the rules to her, but she always knows, she notices everything and asks about everything, *Mummy*, she says, *is there sugar in peanut butter, we're not allowed to bring unhealthy sandwich spreads to kindergarten.*

'You're a very young mother,' he says.

'Yes,' I say.

Then he bends his knees and squats down. He leans forward. He whispers something into her ear.

She nods.

Then she turns her head and whispers something back.

'Let's go now, Alexa,' I say.

She smiles. He smiles, too.

I have never seen her smile like that. And how does she manage to talk to strangers? When I can't manage it at all.

'We're going now,' I say.

She keeps smiling at him, with her mouth shut and her eyes narrowed.

Then I pull her along with me, but she twists around, she waves, and I don't know what I'm going to do now, I don't understand why I'm walking towards the bus stop, we can't take the bus anyway.

'What did he say to you?' I ask.

She doesn't answer.

'Alexa,' I say.

She hops on one foot over a puddle, she is still smiling.

'Answer me now,' I say.

'But Mummy,' she says, and stops hopping. 'It's a secret.'

I stop.

'He's a junkie,' I say. 'You can't have secrets with a junkie.'

Then she pinches her lips together and stares straight ahead.

'What did he say?' I say.

'You told me that you're supposed to keep secrets,' she says.

'But now I'm telling you to answer me,' I say and I say it because something is unravelling now, I squat down, she has never kept any secrets from me before and that feeling comes back now and I can't stand it, I feel like she's going to die and death is actually all over the place, it's just hidden here, it's just covered up with asphalt, and the pharmacy with the cross flashing, but it's just a thin layer and I couldn't bear it if she were to die, I can't bear it that she talks to strangers, I squeeze her shoulders. 'What did he say?' I say.

'That I should . . . but telling secrets is wrong!' she says.

She falls against me and sobs.

'Mummy!' she says. 'And I wet myself, too!'

Her body is completely soft. I hear the bus stopping and the doors opening.

'And my panties are all cold!' she says.

'There, there,' I say.

I hear the doors of the bus closing, and it drives away.

'I always wet myself!' she says.

'Alexa, now,' I say. 'You've been doing very well.'

'And my clothes get all ruined!' she says.

'There, there, little one,' I say.

But she's telling the truth. She wets herself, as much as before, the stickers didn't help, they just agitated her. And her clothes get ruined, she's right about that too, the fabric of some of her panties have become threadbare and discoloured in the crotch.

But now she's talking about other things, her brain just races onward, she's breathing rapidly and shaking her head again.

'And there are so many people who tease one another and he didn't have a hand and at recess I didn't know which jumper to put on!' she says. 'I didn't know which one you said!'

That's how she gets sometimes. Fixated on what I have said.

She really is crazy.

I think that and I have thought it before and it chills me. How could I produce a crazy child? And is it possible to repair her now?

'I pee all the time!' she says and I don't know what to do so I just hold on tight, I just squeeze her close to me and her jacket is cold under my chin and above the shopping centre, the sky is black.

There are some birds perched on top of the neon letters. Now they take flight and rise. They are seagulls. And I remember what Mum said: *If you disturb the nest for the third time, the seagull will never come back.* The raindrops create rings of waves in the puddles. I remember everything Mum said, *the third time you go under, you drown.*

'Nobody likes kids who wet themselves!' Alexa says.

At that I stand up.

I put my hand under her chin.

'Alexa,' I say.

She squeezes her eyes shut.

'Do you know what we're going to do now?' I say. 'We're going to go into the shopping centre there and buy you a pair of panties.'

She opens her eyes.

'Here?' she asks.

'Yes,' I say.

'Now?' she says.

I nod.

Then she starts to laugh.

And I stand there and stare at her. It rains harder, the raindrops splatter on the asphalt around us, but I just want to look at her, I don't know how we are going to get home, how we will find something for dinner, how this weekend will be. I don't have to think about it. Everything will be all right. I brush her hair off her forehead. She is so pretty. The narrow, sparkling eyes, her eyes get like that when she laughs.

And her eyes are the same as his, light blue, and all shining and strange. Her hair is his. And I remember when he found me, it was the last day of school and everyone was outside, everyone was drunk, everyone was lying beside one another on the grass and looking up at the sky and laughing at the clouds, and he fetched a can of beer from the edge of the water and put it in my hand and watched me. And the air smelt of barbecue and I was barefoot, but I wasn't cold, it was the first time I was ever drunk.

Then I went swimming and the water in Vesletjern Pond was black and soft around my body. I was completely white. And he sat on the dam and watched me.

Afterwards the bonfire burnt and I lay in the grass resting my head on a bag, a boy squirted lighter fluid on the flames, I felt everything so clearly and at the same time so faintly, being drunk suited me. Somebody was roasting marshmallows on a stick. I saw how it dripped down into the fire. I raised myself up onto one elbow and drank more. And he sat on a tree stump and watched me.

The sparks flew up towards the sky. It was pretty. Orange and blue.

Then he came over to me and said: 'I've been sitting and watching you all evening. Haven't you noticed?'

'Yes, I have,' I said.

Afterwards some people slept on the grass, a girl was crying over by the dam, then she grew quiet, some people went out into the forest, some rode away on their bikes while singing. But not he and I. We just sat there.

The fire was ash; he poked at it with a stick. Then he put the stick aside.

He said: 'Are you afraid of the dark?'

I said yes.

He said: 'The night isn't dangerous, you know. Night-time is exactly like daytime, just that it's a little dark.'

There was a mist over Vesletjern Pond. I shivered.

But it was just as if it had all happened before. Because I knew what he was going to say.

And he said: 'Are you cold?'

I said yes.

Then he said: 'You can borrow my sweatshirt.'

It was a grey, hooded sweatshirt. He pulled it off. The inside of it was warm, it smelt of fabric softener. Then the birds started singing, first one, then the others, then the motorway began to hum and he opened his mouth and I knew what he was going to say.

'Are you still cold?' he said.

I nodded.

And he said: 'Shall I put my arms around you then?'

And when he touched me, I didn't need to say anything, then we spoke another language that I knew.

In the gym, on the seats on the metro. Beneath the stands and in the grass that was full of withered dandelions. And that autumn at the outdoor court, I sat beneath a maple tree, the leaves were red, I sat with my knees up inside my wool jumper and I never looked at the others, only at him. How his body moved when he was preparing to shoot. How he always made the long-range shots.

Then we went home to his place, it was winter then.

I remember the front door that slammed and our footsteps on the stairs, he opened the door to the flat and inside it was dark.

'Mummy and the others are in Denmark,' he said.

I nodded.

'They won't be back until tomorrow,' he said. 'So you can sleep here.'

'I can't sleep here,' I said. 'Mum is waiting for me at home.'

He closed the door behind us. I put my boots on the shoe rack.

'You can say you're spending the night at a girl-friend's,' he said.

I shook my head. I never spent the night anywhere.

We sat down in the kitchen, he spread Nutella on slice after slice of bread, he always had to eat so much after practice. I sat and looked out the window. All you could see from there was asphalt and low-rise buildings, but I liked asphalt then, and low-rises and parked cars, I was so much in love, I liked everything, the snow and the tyres on the cars, a striped cat that slipped between them. And I thought: this is the only place where I want to be.

The kitchen was yellow and the spice jars were all lined up on top of the range fan.

'Sleep here then, sweetie,' he said.

I remember that flat, how quiet it was, and then the evening came, I remember the hallway and the pillar candle that was there, on the chest of drawers, and it's so strange that it's the same flat, where Alexa comes running out on Sundays now, in his room there were gym clothes lying all over the floor, his old basketball decals pasted in rows on the ceiling, his duvet was all bunched up at one end of the cover.

I stayed over, after all.

But I didn't sleep very much. I lay on Alex's arm and felt his heart beating.

And then it was morning and we sat in the kitchen and ate slices of bread with Nutella, I chewed with my mouth shut and looked out the window. Low-rises, parked cars. The snow was still on the ground. Everything was the same. Everything was different.

That was how she happened.

That was how she was given to me. Like a keepsake, like a jewel. Alexa.

The doors open for us now.

The air smells of perfume. Alexa stops.

There's a Christmas tree beside the escalator, it stretches up through all the floors. Alexa stares. Big packages lie under the tree, some are red, some are gold-coloured, 'Silent Night' is playing from the loudspeakers. I like that song.

Alexa walks towards the tree. I walk beside her. She stops when she's right next to it, she pokes at a silver Christmas ball with her index finger. It bobs. She smiles. And I know that this is right, in a way that nothing was right before. I wondered so much about everything, what everybody was thinking, whether I should say something, whether I should worry about Mum.

But now I know what is right.

It is right to look at this tree. While the choir is singing 'All is calm, all is bright.' It is right to take her by the hand and walk across this floor. Towards mannequins in mini-dresses, into this store, between these racks, along rows of fur coats with a leopard pattern, with Alexa right in front of me and she stares at everything, she touches coat after coat and says, oh, oh, oh.

'Oh, this one's smooth,' she whispers. 'Mummy, feel.'

I feel it. She watches me.

'Yes,' I say. 'This one's very smooth.'

She keeps walking, she turns her head from side to side as she walks. That's how she is. Completely innocent. And I remember when I turned twenty-three and she filled the entire mailbox with flowers, there was pollen on the letters until September, and early this morning, when there was frost on the grass in front of our building, how she squatted down and stared and said 'Mummy, it's almost snow, not quite, but *almost.*'

How she creeps into bed with me at night and whispers, 'Mummy, I'm a little scared.'

And the damp spot from her breath on my throat. When I say: 'The night isn't dangerous, you know. Night-time is exactly like daytime, just that it's a little dark.'

Now she touches a red-sequined dress.

'Mummy,' she whispers. 'Look.'

'How pretty,' I say.

And I remember that I met Karina from my old comprehensive school in the store, she was pushing a shopping cart and had two boys who were screaming and tugging at her hands and Alexa stood in the queue beside me clutching a carton of milk.

Then Karina asked: 'How have you managed not to spoil her?'

I don't know what I answered. But I know what the answer is: Had I been able to, I would have spoiled her so very, very much. A closet full of dresses, the hallway full of fur-lined rubber boots, the shelves full of glitter glue. Because she likes such things. Everything that's soft, everything that's shiny, and now she's touching black boas, thin straps and slips, they slide across her hands and then we spot the children's department.

Alex had shining eyes like that. Like Alexa's are now.

'There,' she says. 'There are the panties.'

She runs ahead of me over to the wall of undergarments. Her reflector dangles.

'Size five years,' she says. 'Or size 110, we have to look, Mummy, I think we have to look a little.'

She's looking already, she's lifting up the garments in the baskets. I can see how she will be as an adult. She will be the kind of mother who finds everything she's looking for, her hands move so quickly, that was how the mothers of the girls in my class were, that's the kind of mother I had planned on being.

'Five years,' she says. 'Size five years.'

She studies the panties. With tiny red bows, with a lace trim and hearts and smiling angels.

I walk over to a rack and look through what's hanging there, the panties are pink, none are in her size, I move on to the purple, the plastic hangers click against one another.

Then I look at the prices.

49. 49. 49.

I go over to one of the baskets.

59.

I move on to the next basket. I start digging. Are there none that are any cheaper? Is this what panties cost? I create a pile. 59, 59, 59, I move to the next basket and dig deeper and unearth all the panties to be found there, but there are only more of the exact same panties, with exactly the same purple little clouds on them, 49, 49, 49, and Alexa scurries around the baskets, *which one shall we take Mummy, which one do you think*?

There have to be more baskets here. There must be a sale. I look around. Pyjamas. Nightgowns.

There aren't any more. There is no sale.

'Maybe one with Tinker Bell on it?' she says and looks up.

Then she blinks. She has noticed it already. That there's something wrong with me.

'Do you like Tinker Bell?' she asks.

I only have 40 kroner.

'Yes,' I say, but my voice sounds strange and I turn away, she walks on along the racks, but I know that she's not looking at the panties, I learnt it at the health clinic: Children will stand with their tummy facing what they feel is safe and their eyes focused on what they're afraid of.

And Alexa is looking at me.

'Or maybe this one, Mummy?' she says and sometimes I just can't bear it, how that word means me, that it's me who's supposed to be Mummy, the one she's calling for all the times she calls out, *Mummy, can you untie this, Mummy, can I sleep with you, Mummy, what are you doing now.*

I do such stupid things. I am not to be trusted. I never have been. I wanted to be, I did, I had thought I would bake and there would be the aroma of fresh-baked bread in the hallway, I would smile at the parents at the kindergarten and always have something to do at the weekends, I would wash Alex's gym clothes and hang them on a clotheshorse. And I dreamt of how Alex would lift Alexa high above him, in the bedroom, with yellow light coming through the window. I remember once he did this. He did, it was in the flat we had before and the sunlight sparkled on the dust in the air and I stood in the doorway of the bedroom and stared at them.

I couldn't really grasp that they were real. That they were mine.

'Or maybe this one is nice?' Alexa says, and I turn towards her and say: 'Yes. That one. Come, let's go into the fitting room.'

She walks in front of me. She is holding the pair of panties in her hand. White with a rainbow pattern.

I can't bear to think any more.

She stops in front of the first fitting room and looks at me. I draw back the curtain and drop her knapsack on the floor.

She unbuttons her trousers and starts to pull them down. I draw the curtain shut.

She smells of urine.

I sit down on a stool. I lean my head against my hands. Then I inhale. I don't know what to do. I look out between my fingers, she's struggling, she's still holding the panties in her hand and trying to pull her trousers further down, they are snug over her long underwear.

'You have to take off your shoes first,' I say.

'Oh,' she says. 'Oh yes.'

I take the panties out of her hand. There is an alarm attached to one side. I twist the panties, Alexa unties her shoes, they have laces, they were cheaper, but she doesn't know how to tie them properly, it takes her a very long time, she's always the last one out when they have recess, it isn't right, the others are already playing when she comes out, I should have thought of that. I do so many stupid things. This is the kind of alarm that howls when you walk out of the store. Alexa kicks off her shoes. I don't know what I am going to do now. She pulls off her trousers and long underwear, she balances on one leg and pulls off one sock.

'That's not necessary, Alexa,' I say. 'Think about it now. Think about what you need to take off to put on a pair of panties.'

She looks down at her body.

I twist the panties again.

Alexa puts the one sock back on. I try pulling at the alarm, the fabric makes a sound. I take my key out of my pocket and poke the end in, under the plastic.

I hear myself swallow. I twist the key, I just try to do something or other, to open up the hole on the inside, to find a mechanism. And then the key slips and hits the plastic and Alexa looks up.

'What are you doing?' she says.

'I'm just looking at the one you chose,' I say.

She pulls the sock on all the way. Then she takes a step towards me.

'But you're ruining it,' she says.

I look down. She's right. She always is. It's not possible to take off the alarm without making a hole in the fabric, and Alexa doesn't like things that are ruined, when the paint colours get mixed together, when the plasticine gets dingy, or the tricycle she had before, she didn't like it that the wheels turned grey, *Mummy*, she said, *can we wash them, I want them to be all white like they were before.*

Now she is staring. At my face, at the panties, back at my face.

'What did you do?' she says.

Her thighs are white and her legs are dry and it's wet on the floor here, she's still wearing the jacket, her legs look so skinny. She always tells the truth. She doesn't understand when you are supposed to lie.

And now she looks at the panties and says: 'There's a hole in it now?'

I close my eyes.

'And we haven't even *bought* it yet,' she says, and I get up and the stool tips over, I drop the panties and pull the curtain aside and the metal rings rattle and her eyes follow me, I know that, I make so many mistakes and she watches me all the time, but I am not to be trusted.

'What are you doing?' she asks. 'Where are you going? Mummy, what are you going to do?'

'I need to get some air,' I say.

26

I walk away, in the direction we came.

'But don't go, I don't have any clothes on!' she says.

I stop.

It's so hot. Drops of sweat run down one side of my abdomen. Behind the counter a girl is sorting clothes hangers. It's so hot and I can hardly breathe and the Christmas carols just play on and on.

'Are you leaving?' Alexa says.

'No,' I say. 'I'm just standing here.'

I have to be calm. I have to grow up. I'm the one she trusts, they say so at the health clinic and it's true. I have to calm down. I stare at the Santa Lucia costumes.

But the flat is too expensive when he doesn't pay and too cold, the floor of the bathroom is as cold as ice under your feet, and Alex, he was always warm and had those shining eyes, but he is looking at other girls now, they are the ones who take care of Alexa, because that's always how I find her, in a corner of the gym and Alex playing guard, because nothing changes, everything is the same, he only scores on fast breaks or from far off, he can't handle it when it gets too crowded, that was what happened when we were living together, he stared at the wall and did the dishes, everything irritated him. And I hate those girls. They sit on a bench with Alexa between their knees and braid her hair, they lend her their earbuds, they throw the ball awkwardly, because they have long fingernails.

But I was the one who sat with him at Vesletjern Pond. I was wearing his sweatshirt, it was the last day of school, the motorway began to hum. It was my blood that he dried off of her body when she was born. But then I come into the gym, and he's playing the way he does, and then the ladies are running around with Alexa and they're wearing singlets and their bra straps are showing and I see him and he stops playing.

'Alexa!' he calls. 'Mummy is here!'

Because I don't talk to those girls there.

I don't want to. I just want to disappear. I just want to go home, but first I have to do everything, and arrange everything, days and dates and times, I have to go to the laundromat and wash panties and add money to the laundry card, and at kindergarten there will be a Christmas breakfast soon and I must pick up and drop off and leave the gym holding Alexa by the one hand and her knapsack in the other, he sends all her clothes back filthy, he doesn't even know how to do a load of laundry or empty the dust filter in the dryer, he doesn't know how to do anything except play basketball and I hate being in the gym, I want to go home.

Where the lunch boxes are drying on the drainer. And the forest is silent outside the kitchen window. That's where I want to go.

I want to be invisible. I don't want to be who I am, Alex's ex, I just want to sit at the kitchen table, and look out at the forest, brown rocks and green moss. Purple heather.

And Alex is always the captain of the team. But lately he hasn't called and asked about her. He thinks it's a long walk from the metro and so often it's raining and the season has begun. He doesn't like to get wet, he has such a weak immune system, he always said that, and I wished that he would get sick so I could buy him Coca-Cola and throat lozenges, but he never got sick and finally he got tired of me, we didn't sleep together every night any more and I couldn't think of anything to say, *you never say anything*, he said, *how am I supposed to know anything about you if you don't talk.*

There are clothes hanging on the hangers. A man crosses the floor. There are things lying on the shelves. The man is carrying a shirt. The walls, the ceiling, the floor. My hands, my trousers, my daughter.

I walk into the fitting room. I set the stool upright, Alexa looks at me. I pull the curtain closed. I sit down.

'Do you want to sit on my lap?' I ask.

She shakes her head. Her eyes dart away and she kneads her feet against the floor, like a kitten, her socks will be completely soaked now.

I place my hand on her arm.

'Alexa,' I say, 'I told a lie.'

'Oh,' she says.

'I was very foolish,' I say.

'No, you weren't, Mummy,' she says.

'Yes,' I say. 'I can't afford it, you see. I can't afford to buy the panties.'

'OK,' she says.

'I just wanted to be nice to you,' I say.

'You are nice, Mummy,' she says.

'But I gave the money to him, the beggar, and Alex, he doesn't send us money any more.'

'That's OK,' she says.

But then I have to look down at the floor, because this, this is exactly what they talk about at the health clinic, *who is supposed to be consoling whom*, they say, and it's exactly the opposite right now, Alexa says, *there, there*, but she doesn't come any closer, I look up through my hair, her mouth is a tiny line, she pats me on the head with a stiff arm and I start babbling now, I notice it, about those days, about the evening at Vesletjern Pond, but she's five years old, but she's big enough, she has to be big enough, because I'm no bigger than this, and I can't stand this, those girls in the gym, I can't stand them, how they talk in baby voices and I am so bad, I am such a bad mother.

'You are not,' Alexa says, and pats my hair. 'My old panties are dry now, for sure. It's fine.'

Her clothes lie strewn all around us.

I look up. Then she opens her mouth.

Then she points.

There are two shoes on the other side of the curtain.

If you disturb the nest for the third time, the seagull will never come back. The third time you go under, you drown. I have known that my whole life.

'Excuse me,' a man says.

Who is this man.

'Come in,' Alexa says.

But I haven't stolen anything. I haven't.

The curtain is drawn aside.

He looks at us. We look back.

'Excuse me,' he says.

A man with a beard. Alexa takes a step backwards. But she doesn't come all the way up against me, not quite, she's so uncertain.

He's wearing a chequered shirt.

Alexa whispers: 'Who is it, Mummy?'

But I don't know who it is. How could anyone know that I was about to steal that pair of panties. And Alexa, she looks so naked wearing just the jacket.

'I didn't mean to listen,' he says.

So he has been listening.

'I was just trying on shirts right next door here,' he says, he points at his shirt.

He has been listening.

'So then I heard what you were talking about,' he says.

'Really?' I say, and I go completely cold, because I hate this, is he going to report me now, to someone or other, to the health clinic, to the police.

'Excuse me,' he says again.

He tries to smile.

'I just wondered,' he said. 'How much does it cost . . . what you want?'

'What does a pair of panties cost?' I say.

His face turns red. And we've only, *I've* only been talking, but he's heard everything, Alexa is the only

32

one I tell the truth to, and now he's heard everything, what happens now, what are we going to do now?

'I wondered if you would consider accepting this?' he asks.

He holds something out to us. A 200-kroner bill. It's quiet now, no Christmas carols, I can hear all the sounds, his breathing, Alexa's jacket, her moves.

'Maybe you need more? It costs more maybe, it's probably not enough?' he says.

'We were just going to buy a pair of panties,' Alexa says, and reaches out her hand. 'They cost 49.'

*

We are sitting in the very front. Alexa looks out at the road. Her eyes twitch, they always do that on the bus. The signal lights tick. I like that ticking sound.

And this evening I am going to sit in the kitchen, with the lights off, I am going to look towards the forest, and everything will be quiet.

'It's almost as if it's night outside,' Alexa says.

I nod.

'Night-time is exactly like daytime,' she says. 'Just that it's a little dark.'

I look at her.

'Do you think there will be frost tomorrow?' she says.

'For sure,' I say.

I look at her. It's her, after all. A girl with finger-prints and a cowlick and ear wax, she had all of that when she was born, I was so young then and I stared at her, I am staring at her still, she was full of things I never would have thought of, sleep in the corners of her eyes and tiny fingernails that curve, she is full of all kinds of things still.

Thoughts I never could have thought.

'Do you think there will be snow?' she says.

'Perhaps,' I say.

The car lights sweep across her face. Dark. Then light. Then dark again.

'I'm sleepy, Mummy,' she says.

'Come here, then,' I say.

I put my arm around her. And then she leans against me. She presses her face up against my jacket and closes her eyes.

THE RIGHT THOMAS

Straight into the pillow shop and straight home and take the food out of the refrigerator.

I am an ordinary man now. I have a plan.

So I walk, down the pavement. But it's already dark and that makes me feel stressed, I wish they could have come earlier, I said so over the phone. *Then we'll be there at six o'clock*, Live said, and I said, *can't you come a little earlier, so he can get used to the flat while it's still light*. But she replied, *Thomas, I have to work until four-thirty. It's winter anyway, it gets dark at three o'clock.*

It's winter anyway.

And people come from all over the place.

They are standing on the pavement playing the accordion, they are running on the pedestrian crossings and carrying huge boxes out of the lamp shop and I am used to knowing who comes out of which door, but now I have no control, their breath is steaming against the cold as they hold kids by the hands, I don't remember the world being so full.

Pay and receive my change and say *have a nice weekend* at the cash register.

And then straight home and take everything out of the refrigerator. I lay in bed reading the recipe all night long, *chop onions and coriander, sauté the onion until it turns golden, place the chicken in the frying pan.*

Because at six o'clock the food has to be ready and I'll open the door and Leon will jump into my arms and Live will smell the aroma and say *what are you preparing?*

Then I answer: 'Lime and coriander chicken.'

Then her eyes will widen.

'Have you eaten?' I will ask.

'Actually I haven't,' she will reply.

And later, when we've eaten and she has said *thank you for a delicious meal* and we have embraced and she has said *see you soon* and she has gone home and I've tucked him in, then I'll sit on the edge of his bed until he falls asleep.

How thin his neck looks. His head on the new pillow.

'Sing the "Stairway" song,' he'll say and he won't be homesick.

Because I remember the last time. I'd borrowed a car from a mate and a cottage from another, the plan was that Leon would whittle a bow and arrow and swim in the river and in the evening we would walk home carrying our fishing poles over our shoulders and then I would place my hand on his neck and explain everything.

That plan went down the drain.

Because the light didn't come into the cottage properly and he was full of homesickness, so I couldn't bring myself to say anything at all, we just played Ludo until it was impossible to tell the difference between blue and green and then I put him to bed. But ten minutes later he stuck his head out over the edge of the loft.

'I can't sleep,' he said.

'Why not?' I said.

'You have to put away the trolls,' he said.

'What trolls?' I said.

'The ones standing on that shelf,' he said.

He pointed. There were two carved trolls on the mantle.

'You can't see them from up there,' I said.

'No,' he said. 'But I'm thinking about them.'

So I got up and took down the trolls and put them in the bottom of a chest.

And then I sat down at the table with a beer. But five minutes later I heard his voice again.

'I know they're in here,' he said.

I looked up. His head was sticking out.

'What?' I said.

'I know the trolls are here. I heard that you didn't go outside,' he said.

'Yes,' I said. 'But you can't see them.'

'Can't we throw them out?' he asked.

'They aren't mine,' I answered.

He stared down at me.

'But I can put them outside in the forest,' I said.

So I took the trolls out of the chest and went out and put them in the car.

That's how dumb I was.

Now I am somebody else, an ordinary man.

And there's the street corner. And there's the sign for the pillow shop, and there's the pub, it's only four o'clock, I have plenty of time, but I make proactive choices, I walk right past the tables outside and into the car park, my gaze is fixed on the pillow shop.

That's where I'm headed.

*

Silk Sleep mattress topper. JYSK junior duvet. Beds and curtains and placards of people fast asleep, shelves full of things I have no idea what are.

I just have to get a handle on this.

I put my hand on a bedpost, *your breathing is an anchor, breathe calmly when you are feeling stressed.* I take ten deep breaths.

Then I let go of the bedpost. I look around, more slowly. There are too many fucking pillows here.

But there's the counter, in the middle of the room and there's a girl standing beside the till, her hair is straight and black, she notices me, she smiles. I walk towards her and smile back.

I have lived in the world for thirty-three years. I know how to buy a pillow.

She has brown eyes, she looks directly at me.

'I would like to buy a pillow,' I say. 'For my son.'

'So you want a child's pillow then?' she asks.

But I haven't thought about that and now it starts, it happens so bloody fast, I have been out for thirty hours and already I'm feeling suffocated, but I remember what she said, she sat on the other side of the table and behind her were potted plants and there was a picture of a beach hanging on the wall and she held her notepad in her hand and said: 'But this business of feeling suffocated. Can you talk a little more about that?'

I'd been seeing her for a while then. I managed to sit still and think there.

'It's because I get insecure,' I said.

'And when do you get insecure?' she asked.

'When people attack me,' I answered.

'But I mean, when do you feel that people attack you?' she asked.

'When they *do*,' I answered, but she wouldn't give up, she never did, she said I should speak about *specific situations*, and then I noticed that I hated to talk about such situations, it made me remember too much, how he carried on, his eyes that were everywhere, on everything I did and the letters I wrote, and they were almost always wrong, so I made my handwriting smaller and smaller so nobody would see, *are those supposed to be letters or mouse droppings, is that what you call doing the dishes*, I hate specific, it makes me feel too much and the way he had of asking about things, *tell me about the Industrial Revolution*, and my thoughts grew hot and I knew that everything I was going to say was wrong, how he said *go to your room*, I couldn't bear to talk about him, I had to choose something else.

'Like when the prison officers say *move it*,' I said.

'Yes,' she said.

'That's how you talk to dogs,' I said.

'Do all the prison officers talk like that?' she asked.

'Mostly the short blonde one,' I replied.

'Oh dear,' she said, and wrote something down on her notepad.

'So I get like that . . . when people have power or something,' I said. 'When they look down on me or something.'

She stood up and switched on a lamp in the corner.

'But are you sure they're looking down on you?' she asked.

'Yes,' I said. 'I can feel it.'

'Exactly,' she said. 'You can *feel* it.'

She stood there with her hand on the lamp cord and looked at me. And I understood what she meant.

That it wasn't necessarily true.

She smiled at me.

She understood that I understood.

She sat down.

'So the question becomes: how can you address that insecurity,' she said. 'Do you have any suggestions for what you can do?'

And I had suggestions. Because I was so smart in there, it was as if I had a new brain there, there I became kind and wise, out here I am dumb and the light from the fluorescent bulbs is harsh against my skin, I am pale and I don't like being pale, I haven't had a chance to get to a tanning salon.

I look at the black-haired girl. She is wearing an apron and has a name tag on her chest.

'I'm sorry,' I say. 'Aysha. What did you ask me?'

'You want to buy a child's pillow?' she says.

But this isn't an attack. This is just something I don't master, if you've felt under attack for your entire life, this is how you react, *that is Stone Age biology*, the psychologist said, *the fear is embedded in the brain*, but I'm not going to behave like a caveman, because I live in a time period with pillow shops and psychologists and traffic lights and if I continue to feel suffocated and lose it, then the same thing will happen to Leon, my father scared the bejesus out of me, and I scare the bejesus out of him, but I don't want to.

I want Leon to sleep peacefully in his bed.

I want him to go to school and walk up to the teacher's desk and show the whole class his cursive handwriting. I want him to be master of ceremonies for the Christmas pageant and stand in front of the curtain and say *how nice that you all came out tonight*, I want him to become an adult and open glass doors with a key card and sit down behind a desk and answer the phone, and say, *yes, we can do that for you.*

And earn hundreds of thousands a year and pay taxes.

So I have to be honest.

'Excuse me?' Aysha says.

'To tell you the truth,' I say, 'I don't know all that much about pillows.'

Then she looks up at me and smiles.

'But we'll find what you need,' she says. 'I can take you around and show you some options.'

She opens a little door in the counter and smiles so I will step aside. She walks in front of me between the shelves, her hair is black and shiny, I don't feel suffocated now, she has an apron wrapped around her waist and her ass moves from side to side, that ass is perfect in relation to the body, and I can't forget Live, she walked up the stairs, she had taken off her sandals and was carrying them in her hand, her hair was wet from the rain, she hummed that karaoke song. She unlocked the door to the flat. She lived on the top floor and I'd never been there before.

That such random things.

That they can change everything.

There you are, wandering down Karl Johan Street just looking for your mates, you check pub after pub, but you don't find any familiar faces, so you go to a karaoke bar and then you meet Live.

And in prison everyone sat talking about their exes, the ladies who always win in court, they stand there speaking in their girlish voices and say *he was never there when I was pregnant*, and in prison the guys bent over the carpenter's bench and changed the sandpaper and explained, different men, but the same story over and over again, they get out and go to pick up their kids and ring the doorbell and the house is empty with dark windows, the ladies have just gone away, the junk mail is piled up on the door-mat and the guys are left standing outside in their sneakers, because they were sent to prison in the summertime and meanwhile the ladies have found new boyfriends whom the children call daddy.

I know that it's true, too.

That's the kind of ladies I used to be with before. I know how it would have been.

She would have stood in the doorway to the sit-ting room holding the child in her arms and said foul things and I would have got up from the couch and slammed the door and charged down the stairs and she would call me and I wouldn't pick up and I would be with my mates and fall asleep in front of the telly and she would call me again and I would answer and she would say: 'Shouldn't you be at home with your girlfriend and your son?'

Instead I had a child with Live.

She reads books and her hair falls down over her eyes. She reads until it grows dark, leaning over the kitchen table. She understands everything. And for-gives everything.

But I don't understand her. And I don't know her.

And I had just walked down Karl Johan Street looking for my mates, but everyone was away on holiday, it was muggy and I got all sweaty under my T-shirt, and finally I reached the karaoke place at the end of the street. The door was wide open. I entered in the middle of a song and went over to the bar. I ordered a beer and put both my hands around the glass. It felt good.

There were three women on stage, and people sitting at a couple of the tables. I didn't know anyone there.

But by the wall, all the way up in the front, near the stage, sat Live.

She was sitting alone. Above her hung a black and white picture of a trumpet. She was concentrating, I could see that, she stared at the stage the whole time and her face changed with the music.

I can't explain what it was about her. But I couldn't stop myself from looking. It was her body and hair, her facial expressions, all of it.

I took my glass and got to my feet.

I walked through the room and sat down at the table next to hers.

Then the song was over. She smiled then, and clapped hard and fast. The women remained on stage, they leaned over and spoke with her and the DJ said: 'Anyone else want to have a go?'

Nobody responded.

'Then we'll do "Preacher Man",' one of the women said.

The DJ put on the music and the women started singing again. They sang like kindergarten teachers actually, they wore glasses and swayed their hips and snapped their fingers, but they were good, you aren't supposed to sing so great at a karaoke bar.

So some people left, others turned away. But not Live.

She rubbed her arms. Her foot bobbed in time with the music. She was wearing sandals with thin leather straps. And the entire woman, I don't know. The entire woman was golden.

'Are they your friends, those women?' I asked.

'Yes,' she said.

'Aren't you getting up there?' I asked.

She looked at me.

'No,' she said.

Then there was a clap of thunder and the lights went out and the loudspeakers went dead, but we could hear the song without the music, because her friends just smiled and kept singing.

I turned around and outside the door the rain started pouring down, somebody ran past holding a newspaper over their head, then the power came back on and the music started up again, the women shrugged their shoulders and kept singing, Live kept watching and I kept sitting beside her and smiling when she smiled, clapping when she clapped, just as much as she did. Then the song was over.

'Are you sure you're not going to sing?' I asked.

'I can't sing,' she answered.

'Shall we dance then?' I asked and then she looked over at her girlfriends and at me and at the empty dance floor. There was another clap of thunder, out on the street somebody screamed and the lights in the ceiling blinked.

'Yes,' she said. 'Why not.'

Her friends sang. We danced alone. And it thundered so the floor shook, the music went on and off and her body was narrow and unfamiliar and nice, but finally the DJ was fed up and said: 'All these power outages, the system's gonna break down.'

And then her friends went home, but the two of us went to another bar and danced some more and afterwards we went to her place and had sex, she

liked how I danced and what I said and how we had
sex, she turned her back to me when we were finished, and took my arm and laid it over her and the
next morning I had a headache, then she went into
the bathroom and came back with a glass of water
in one hand and two pills in the other

'Here you go,' she said. 'You may as well take
two right away.'

I raised myself up on my elbow and nodded.

Then I swallowed and lay there under the duvet
and tried to understand where it was I'd ended up.

White curtains. A summer dress hanging from
the curtain rod. A picture of Saturn over the bed, in
the middle of black outer space.

And I'd never in my entire life taken less than
four aspirin tablets.

It was only then that I understood that I'd come
to a completely different planet.

Now Aysha stops. I stop, too. I look where she's
looking.

A woman walks out of a door. She is carrying a
stack of something in her arms. Aysha lifts her hand
and fiddles with her name tag.

'You know what,' she says. 'Somebody else
should help you now.'

'Oh,' I say.

'Because I'm really supposed to be at the till,' she says. 'But ask her, she'll give you the help you need.'

Then Aysha sneaks past me, along the shelves, but the other woman sees her anyway and then she calls out: 'Why aren't you at the till?'

'There wasn't anybody else to help him' Aysha says and she runs to the till and the woman shakes her head and places the stack on a bed, and comes towards me.

'Yes?' she says.

Short, grey hair and those kinds of glasses. Is she the one who is going to help me? One of those people who sees everything.

But this is what people do, buy pillows, talk to strangers. And other people don't let it bother them the way I do, they don't lose their entire self through a hole in themselves, that's not how they feel.

They just say something. They just say what they want.

'I'd like to buy a pillow for my son,' I say.

'Down, feather or synthetic?' the lady says and I notice that I'm sweating now, for sure I already smell of sweat and I see what she sees, when she looks at me, who I am, where I have been.

Down, feather or synthetic.

She just wonders what kind of pillow I want.
*Look inside other people's heads. See their version
of things.*

'I don't know,' I say.

'You don't know?' she says.

She raises her eyebrows.

Then she walks right past me and I follow her,
because this is the kind of experience you must tol-
erate, people have their reasons, my father had his,
this lady has hers, and I remember what the psychologist said: 'Do you have any suggestions for what
you can do?'

I got so smart in there.

'Can I borrow your pen?' I asked.

She leaned across the table and handed me her
pen. I took it and wrote on the back of my hand.

'Why.'

That was it. Then the session was over.

And the next time there was lock-up, I was ready,
move it, the prison officer yelled, it was the short
blonde one, I was standing in the hallway and talking
with a neighbour, I heard the footsteps and the rattling, door after door slamming shut. I turned my

back to the prison officer and looked down at the back of my hand.

'Hey!' he said. 'Kristiansen! Move it! Into the cell!'

I turned around. Behind him was the hallway, long and empty and green.

'Why do you say it like that?' I asked.

'What?' he said.

'I'm not a dog,' I said.

Then I walked into the cell.

And I wasn't stressed and I wasn't angry. I didn't feel suffocated.

Why.

That's the best answer.

It forces people to look into themselves. And what they see there is not always something they like. Then they quiet down for a while.

'Standard, queen or king?' she says.

But she doesn't turn around.

'What?' I say.

'*Standard, queen* or *king*,' she says, but she still doesn't turn around, she keeps walking in those black shoes of hers and those wide hips and just speaks louder, as if I'm deaf or an idiot and my back straightens up now, my legs move faster.

Then I am right behind her.

I place my hand on her arm.

She stops.

I have been hollered at enough in my life, that's the thing, I have been treated like I'm deaf or an idiot often enough.

She turns around.

She is wearing red lipstick and square glasses and what irritates me is that *she* can be cheeky, people like her, who have a job and a house and a husband and for fourteen months I've been lying in a narrow bed and staring at the ceiling and yearning for everything and here she comes and has been out in the world all this time and wants to put me down, it makes me angry and I don't manage to stop the anger, because it comes like high tide and forces its way in everywhere, but in my head I can hear, *is that so*, says the psychologist, *and do you have any suggestions for what you can do then?*

I take my hand away from her arm.

'Why do you say it like that?' I ask.

'What?' she says.

'Why are you yelling at me?' I ask.

It works.

She looks into herself. And I can breathe. I can think.

Leon's head on the pillow. That everything will be as it was, as it has never been, as it should be.

But then she sighs.

'Well, this won't be easy,' she says. 'You don't know what kind of pillow you want and you don't know anything about materials?'

'No,' I say.

'Do you know anything about price range?' she says.

My fists clench, I open them again.

'No,' I reply.

Then she breathes in through her nose.

'How old is your son?' she asks. 'Perhaps that's a place to start?'

How old is your son.

How old is your son. I know the answer to that. If there is one thing I remember it's the day he was born, the snow had started to melt and it was dripping from all the rooftops when I went up to the maternity ward and there he lay, in a Plexiglas box and he smiled at me, if there is one thing I care about it's his birthday, I was granted a prison furlough to go to the toy store, I sent him a Lego helicopter and a plastic wolf, I sent it two weeks early to be sure it arrived in time, but my brain is a blank slate right now and I know why, it's stress in the frontal lobe, it causes the memory to stop working, and I am sweaty and it stinks, and when she looks at me like that, with that hairdo and that mouth, then I have no clue, my brain doesn't work, I'm like how I was when I was a little boy. I have no idea how old Leon is.

And it feels like the room is tilting now, that it starts to glide in a circle around us, curtains and sheets, special offer, special offer, sale. But in the midst of it all, she is standing there and she doesn't move at all.

'I don't know,' I say.

Now everything tips back towards me. I lift my hand and hold onto a shelf.

'You don't know how old your child is?' she says.

Then she smiles.

And I have to get out of there.

Because some things are an attack. That smile there is an attack. But I am somebody else now, I don't react to stuff like that, I don't make trouble, that's not how I am any longer.

So then I turn around and walk away.

I don't knock anything over, I don't throw anything, I just turn around, I just walk away.

*

And then I'm outside, I run across the car park and reach the street, I stop and catch my breath, the street lamps are glittering and the cars are driving slowly out into the intersection and the brake lights shine red and there's the pub and a beer is the last thing I need right now, a beer is exactly what I need right now, and my feet walk, I'm a new man now, I go into the city centre and buy a pillow there. Because in an hour and a half, Leon will come, and I walk between chairs and outdoor tables, but there's the door I'm not going to enter, I stop, I stand there looking at the door, it's of dark glass, a light is on above it, I met Live at a place like this, but what was Live doing in such a place, I remember such places, how the world disappears when the door closes behind you.

Now is the time when I must demonstrate that everything is a choice. Not choosing is also a choice.

Now I have to think about how it was, about how it can be once more.

What Live looks like. Those eyes of hers. When she looked at me for a long time and handed me two aspirin tablets and a glass of water.

Then she took teacups out of the cupboard and I sat at the kitchen table, her legs were naked under her bathrobe. She went into the lavatory and I heard her peeing and I felt embarrassed. There was a radio on the windowsill and I turned it on so I wouldn't hear the sound, there was opera on the radio. When that song was over, something new started, there were violins, I leaned forwards, the words on the display read NRK Classical.

Ladies like that. Radio stations like that. I didn't even know they existed.

Then I heard her footsteps crossing the floor, she opened and closed the front door. She came back with a newspaper in her hand and asked which section I wanted.

'Section?' I said.

'Financial?' she said. 'Or news or culture?'

'Culture,' I said.

She handed me half the newspaper and then I understood what she was talking about, but I've never slept with a woman who wanted to sit in the kitchen reading the newspaper the next day, or somebody who shook tea into a tea strainer and looked out of the window and said *look, what nice weather*. And everything was so peaceful there. The table was up against the window, the steam rose white out of the tea cups. A clock without hands was hanging on the wall, in the middle of the clock there was only the word *now*.

She turned her face towards the window. Her throat was slender.

'Look, what nice weather,' she said. 'But we can't be bothered to go for a walk or anything.'

'A walk?' I said.

'No,' she said. 'I guess we're too tired for that.'

And then she yawned and bent over the newspaper.

I looked at her kitchen. The oven with yellow lights on it. The kitchen counter made of wood. By the cooker there was a bell jar full of oatmeal, on the windowsill she had a spice plant, on the refrigerator hung a piece of paper with the words *Recycling in your neighbourhood* on it.

'Are you looking at my kitchen?' she said.

'Yes,' I said.

'Why's that?' she said.

'I just had to see,' I said, 'how you live.'

'How I live?' she said and folded the newspaper once and started looking around. 'Well, what do you think?' she asked.

'Very nice,' I answered.

The oven emitted a soft beep and she stood up, put in a baking sheet and said *ten minutes, then the rolls will be ready.* She got into the shower and I leafed through the newspaper, back and forth.

Then I looked outside. Two little girls were playing Chinese jump rope down on the footpath. They had tied the jump rope to a bench, and after a while the oven beeped again and she opened the bathroom door and called: 'Can you please take the rolls out and slice them? There's a knife in the top drawer.'

I stood up.

'I'm just going to get dressed,' she said.

So I stood there with the potholders in my hands and warm rolls on a wire rack. Like another kind of man. In another kind of life.

When she came back, I had sliced the rolls and found plates, she came in wearing sweatpants and a T-shirt, I stood there holding one plate in each hand. She took the cold cuts out of the refrigerator. And me, I had absolutely no sense of timing. Because that's when I said: 'Can I see you again?'

'See me?' she said.

'Yes,' I said.

Her hair was wet. There were dark blotches on her T-shirt.

'I don't mind,' she said.

She sat down at the table and reached out her hands. I gave her the plate.

'I'm so hungry,' she said. 'We should have had eggs and bacon, too.'

I sat down.

She spread butter on the roll and sliced cheese and chewed and swallowed, but after a while she looked up and then she saw that I sat there staring.

'Yes,' she said. 'Yes, we can see each other again.'

Then she held the roll directly above the plate and looked at me.

'But I don't want a boyfriend or anything like that,' she said. 'Just so you know. Yes, just so I've said it.'

'OK,' I said.

'I'm sure you don't want that either,' she said. 'I mean, like, you know.'

'I understand,' I said. 'But we can see each other all the same?'

She nodded. But she looked sceptical. And I got the picture. So I sat there for a while pretending to read the newspaper, breakfast was over, the only option was to put on my shoes, the only option was to give up, because she put the plates in the sink and hummed, *and the only one who could ever reach me, was the son of a preacher man*, she didn't ask for my phone number, she read the weather report on the last page of the newspaper and when I left, she just gave me a hug and said *nice meeting you, Thomas.*

So I gave up.

I left, down the stairs and out the door, I thought it was a dream, the rolls and the morning and the night, a golden lady like that. I tried to forget about her in different ways and new days came and nights and new ladies and after a few weeks she was like a dreamt dream, I didn't think about her all the time any longer, but one month later she was the one who called and said: 'Thomas?'

'Yes,' I said.

'I don't know if this is the right Thomas,' she said.

'What?' I said.

'I don't know if this is the right Thomas,' she said and her voice was faint, but then I recognized it.

'Yes,' I said. 'This is the right Thomas. Hello again.'

But then she started to cry.

She had been to The Trumpet and asked about me. First, the bouncer and the DJ and the bartender, but they didn't know, and then she sat there four nights in a row and drank apple juice and asked everyone who came in whether they knew somebody named Thomas, and everyone there knew somebody or other named Thomas, *and it was bloody humiliating*, she said later, *they understood immediately what had happened.*

'They can't possibly have understood,' I said.

'Yes, I could feel it,' she said. 'But what was I supposed to do?'

So what she did was get the phone numbers of everyone named Thomas and call them and say *I don't know if this is the right Thomas. But were you at The Trumpet one month ago?*

And the first six had said no, but she wondered whether the last two had fibbed to avoid seeing her again, *you should have seen me*, she said, *I sat in the kitchen and chewed my fingers and had no idea what to do* and she had eight different Thomases to call but the seventh of these was me.

'This is the right Thomas,' I said. 'Hello again.'

And then she started crying and then I also understood what was what.

What it was, was Leon. And that's why I'm leaving now.

So I turn around. I can feel the pub behind my back.

But I have a plan, I'm going to buy a pillow, so it won't be like the last time, when I sat in that dark cottage, I don't know how many times he stuck his head over the edge of the loft, my thoughts got all mixed up in my skull, it happened again and again.

'When are you going to bed?' he asked.

'I don't know,' I answered.

'Mum goes to bed at eleven,' he said.

'Yes,' I said. 'Close your eyes now, Leon.'

'I can't,' he said.

His eyes were big. His hair was tousled.

Then I climbed up the ladder and crept into the loft. I was tipsy. But I felt that things were as they should be all the same.

'Somebody usually sings until I fall asleep,' he said.

'You don't say,' I said.

'And I don't have a pillow,' he said.

I pulled off my sweater and placed it under his head.

And then I sang 'Stairway to Heaven'. Verse after verse after verse while I patted his hair and the ceiling was so low there, I had to sit with my head cocked to one side.

'What's it about?' he asked.

'About a stairway,' I answered.

'What do you smell like?' he asked.

'Nothing,' I answered and then I went on singing.

He fell asleep in the end.

But the next morning he was very tired.

When we drove back he had to pee, so I parked the car in a bus bay and got out, I rubbed my face, we were so tired, I shivered. I placed my hand on his neck.

'Look,' I said.

'Horses,' Leon said.

And I couldn't bring myself to tell him that I was going to prison. I couldn't bring myself to say good-bye. Not when he looked so skinny and tired.

We just stood there, by the electric fence and stared at the horses, until it started to rain.

Then I drove him home again.

But I'm different now. I remember when I was little and we walked past the junkies, *they have no plan,* my father said, every time, but I have a plan now, I am going to take the streetcar, right into the city centre and buy a pillow and then straight home and take the chicken out of the refrigerator.

I take one step forward.

Then I hear something. It is a door opening, I take one more step, I look straight ahead, *proactive choices*, but I feel something else.

A hand on my arm.

'Well, hello,' a voice says. 'Thomas!'

*

I turn around.

Blonde hair and round cheeks. A big smile. A tight singlet and a knitted jacket over her arm.

'Don't you recognize me?' she says. 'Vibeke?'

This always happens.

I can see her breath like mist coming out of her mouth. She starts to pull on the knitted jacket and says: 'From comprehensive school?'

She smells of beer, she smiles the whole time. I can't remember any girl like her in my class. She sticks her hand in her pocket and takes out a pack of cigarettes.

'Vibeke,' I say. 'Of course I remember you.'

'Yes, I've put on a little weight,' she says. 'But it should be possible to recognize me even so?'

Then she laughs. She has a gold heart on her eye tooth. She is standing in the glow from the light above the door. She bows her head and lights the cigarette, she looks up again. She's nice and tan; she's scantily dressed for the weather.

'But are you living here again now or what?' she says.

'I've moved into my mother's old apartment,' I answered. 'It's temporary.'

'Then we'll be neighbours again,' she says. 'But are you on the way out or the way in? You're standing like sideways?'

'I'm actually on my way home,' I say.

But I get so restless at home, I just keep walking in circles. I cleaned everything yesterday, I filled the refrigerator, I memorized the recipe last night, now the bed is made and the Ludo game is set up on the table, I can't like touch anything. I look at the clock above the intersection, the numbers glow red.

It won't be six o'clock for a long time.

'But I could smoke a cigarette with you?' I say.

'That would be nice,' Vibeke says.

And I act like I am searching my pockets until she says *do you want one?* and holds the pack out to me. I thank her and pull out a pink lighter and a smoke and I have to struggle to light it, the lighter is so small and my fingers are cold, it's been a long time since I've smoked, I get tears in my eyes, I turn away so she won't see, the wind is blowing and I can smell how the air has the scent of winter, *there's snow in the air*, my father said, he was different then, we stood on the shore below my grandmother's house, he could relax there, there was nobody who saw what a failure I was.

I turn back. Her throat is so bare. It makes me want to put a scarf there.

'Are you cold?' I ask. 'Do you want to borrow my jacket?'

'Wow,' she says. 'I don't need it. But thanks.'

She smokes quickly, she trembles a little bit. I shouldn't have said that stuff about my jacket, I have such bad timing, I'm out of practice.

Then she turns her back to me and carefully stubs out the cigarette against the stone wall, her skirt is tight and black, I don't remember anybody like this named Vibeke. She puts the smoke back into the pack again and says:

'I'm trying to quit, you see.'

'How's that going?' I say.

'Halfway there,' she says. 'I smoke half a cigarette instead of a whole one.'

Then I smile and she holds my gaze, for a long time.

This I know how to do.

And I remember Live, we danced until all the bars closed, then we stood there on Storting Street and it was four o'clock and the birds were twittering and I said: 'I'm not leaving you alone here. Shall I walk you home?'

Then she gave me a look.

'I can pay your taxi fare, if you'd rather,' I said.

Even though I didn't have any money for any taxi.

'No,' she said. 'You can walk me home.'

Now Vibeke has that look. I finish my cigarette. She is looking at me the whole time.

'I remember you well,' she says.

I nod.

'You wore jeans to the school formal,' she says.

I nod again.

'And weren't you the one who set the baby Jesus on fire?' she asks.

'Not the baby Jesus,' I say.

'Oh?' she says.

'Just the hay in the manger,' I say.

Then she laughs and says, *yeah, there's a big difference when the entire end-of-term pageant has to be evacuated*, and I laugh too. We are standing beneath a small overhang. I lean to one side and stub out the cigarette in an ashtray.

'I'm just waiting for someone,' she says. 'You want to come in for a while?'

Then she smiles again and opens the door for me.

*

I remember why I like pubs. I like to walk down the stairs. I like that it's warm inside and that the ladies sit on barstools, and it's dark and you have to lean forwards to talk to people, I like it when they turn up the music so you have to lean in even closer. And I like the kind of bartenders like this one here, he just nods, he doesn't ask where I've been, I sit down, I lean my elbows on the bar. I remember that I like that too.

Vibeke pulls off her knitted jacket. She is wearing a watch with a pink strap. I take her hand and turn it towards me. Ten minutes to five.

'Are you going somewhere soon?' she says.

I shake my head. She puts the pack of cigarettes on the bar.

'I have to quit,' she says.

I nod.

'It's only white trash who smoke now,' she says.

'White trash?' I say.

'Don't you know what that is?' she asks.

I shake my head. But now my throat is starting to thud. It doesn't take much. Because I know who's white trash, it's people like me and I understand who calls people such things, teachers and Live's girl-friends, my father, the entire system, but the system is no system, it's a cognitive error, I have to remember that, but I thought actually that I was going to see a psychologist to be consoled, so I sat in the chair and talked a little about the trial and my shitty lawyer, and after a while I ran out of things to say, so I talked about how I hated the system and that the system was not for me. But then she leaned forwards and asked: 'What is this system you keep talking about?'

And I said: 'The system that has failed me.'

And she said: 'But specifically, Thomas, who is it that you feel has failed you?'

'My mum,' I said. 'My father. All of them.'

'You mean your family?' she said.

'Not really,' I said. 'I mean the education system and the whole package.'

'Hmm,' she said.

'And the correctional services, not least,' I said.

And she asked: 'Do you mean the government?'

'No,' I answered.

But I did mean something or other, about something that bothered me, people, that people just dream about the same things and follow rules when they don't know why they exist, and get the best grades all the time and report people to the police and are proud of it, I meant something like that.

'I mean my parents and all of Norway and everything,' I said.

'So you mean the human race,' she said.

'Yes,' I said.

'And what is your alternative?' she said.

'What?' I said.

'Where are you going to live?' she said. 'If you're fed up with the human race.' Then I looked at her. Because my arguments unravelled like an old sweater. But she just sat there and looked back at me with those small glasses of hers in front of those green plants of hers and I felt that I fell, I fell, backwards.

What is the alternative?

I live in the world, after all.

And the world, that's not a system. It's just some people.

So I went back to my cell and didn't sleep a wink that night.

I didn't even try to go to bed. I wandered back and forth across the floor and thought, further and further inside myself, I thought about my own thoughts and I noticed how they were, they just drove around in their own tracks, like the hot wheel cars I had when I was little. I walked until morning came.

The sun rose above the fields outside.

And I turned my back to the window. I stopped.

Above my bed hung the drawing Leon had sent. I stood there looking at it.

A green line for the grass, a blue line for the sky. A house and three people.

And the sunlight fell upon the drawing, like a frame.

Then something clicked inside my head.

The strange light and the drawing. The people and the house. And the sky was like so far away from the grass. It looked like the people were just floating in the air.

I can't explain it. But that's when I decided.

To become somebody else.

To have a plan.

Now Vibeke places her hand on my forearm. There are some women who do things like that, they touch people, but she doesn't know how long it's been since somebody touched me, it disturbs me, my arm stiffens.

'So,' she says. 'How've you been since I saw you last?'

'Kind of up and down,' I say.

'Yes, that's life,' she says.

And that's true.

I don't know if she really knows it, but that's how life is, a bleeding ocean, you get in so deep, and then you're flung out again, and suddenly you're lying there on the beach swallowing salt water and starfishes all by yourself, and suddenly you are riding on the top of a wave and everything around you is sparkling, and the highest peaks were those times with Live, but that was almost not me, it was almost another man and the deepest troughs were the first weeks in prison, then I was at rock bottom, I lit both lights in the cell, but everything was completely black all the same. And during the daytime it was day, but it was dark then too, from the moment the prison officer opened the vision panel and shouted *good morning*, my body didn't want to get out of bed, my hand didn't want to lift the electric razor, I felt the water that rose up in my throat and I went to that job and built chairs for other prisoners in other prisons, but the dark water rose in the course of the day and when the time came for lock up, I just sat on my bed and let it rise, I knew that the night was a done deal, every night I lay there and floundered through the darkness, impossible to get out of it. I knew. I hadn't even said goodbye to Leon. I had cocked up so bad.

And I just couldn't manage to do anything about it.

'Anyway, it's nice seeing you again,' Vibeke says.

'Thanks,' I say.

'Thanks,' she says, but not to me, because now her beer is on the bar, she hands the bartender a banknote and he winks at her, he has a new hairstyle, his bangs are long and slanted.

I am an ordinary man now. I have a plan.

Then he looks at me.

And if there's one thing I know how to do, it's this. If there's one thing I know how to do, it's how to give up.

'*You have choices all the time,*' the psychologist said. '*Not choosing is also a choice.*'

'And you,' the bartender says. 'What are you having, boss?'

I look at Vibeke's watch. It's just five.

I nod towards Vibeke's glass.

'I'll have one of those,' I say.

*

An ordinary man is able to go into a pub and then buy a pillow and get home by six o'clock.

The bartender holds the glass under the tap.

'Forty-nine kroner,' he says, he puts the beer on the bar and I see the psychologist, she leans forwards, it looks like she thinks this is a bad idea.

But I'm not going back to see her, she gave me a hug and said *good luck now, Thomas,* and it feels like it was many years ago, but it was the day before yesterday and I will never go there again, I'm alone now and she also said that life doesn't have to be either–or, so why can't an ordinary man have a beer with friends, I pull out my wallet and hand the bartender a banknote and a yellow Post-it drops down onto the bar.

It's my handwriting. *Coriander*, *chicken*, and then I can't see what's written there, in my miniature handwriting.

But he's given me the beer now.

He places the change on the bar.

'I'll have a coffee, too,' I say.

'Say what?' the bartender says.

'I think I need a coffee first,' I say. 'To wake me up a little.'

Then he nods and reaches towards the cups, they are hanging from a beam. I put the shopping list back in my wallet.

Because Leon, he is never going to write in such tiny handwriting. He is going to write large, clear letters, and here comes the coffee and I'm not going to have that beer, I will leave it there, because I know what's important to me, to be home by six o'clock, and now Vibeke has her hand on my arm again.

'And you?' she says. 'You look sort of gobsmacked.'

She straightens her back, her boobs stick out more.

'Hmm?' she says. 'Did you just arrive from another planet?'

Hiding things doesn't help. You always know what you've hidden. I put my hands around the coffee cup.

'To tell you the truth,' I say. 'I was in prison for a while.'

'Oh,' she says.

Then she smiles.

'It's good to get some life experience,' she says.

She leans her head to one side.

'But I don't remember you being so quiet, exactly,' she says.

'No,' I say.

'Tell me something, then,' she says.

'Like what?' I say.

'The story of your life?' she says. 'But I have to go to the loo first. Will you wait?'

I nod.

Then she slides down off the barstool. She pulls her skirt down as she walks.

*

The story of my life. It makes no sense at all. The only thing he wanted was for me to be a proper son and my mother, the only thing she wanted was for my father to have his way, and then it all went so completely to hell that you would think it was a fairy tale. Then I became the person I became, the one who clogged up the toilets in primary school with towels, the third shepherd who filled the entire Christmas pageant with smoke, the one who ended up in prison and I know what the neighbours said then, *it had to happen, I could have told you so.*

I've like lived so many lives.

All the forgotten days and all the days I remember.

When the snow melted and I went to the hospital and Leon was lying there smiling. When the psychologist said *what is your alternative, where are you going to live?* And long before that, when I was the seventh one named Thomas and Live called and said that I was going to be a father, she said we had to meet and talk about it, and it was as if God had opened up the entire sky and just dropped the finest things right on top of me.

So I went there the next day. I went to the entrance, I pressed the doorbell.

'Just a second,' she said. 'I'll be right down.'

I waited on a bench. The windows in the building were open, I could smell that somebody was frying pork chops. The bench was green, the paint was peeling off. It took a while. Then she came. She was as I remembered and she was standing in front of me.

'I thought, we have to get to know each other,' she said.

She sat down beside me.

'What kind of work do you do?' she asked.

'Right now I'm between jobs,' I said.

Then she nodded and sucked her lower lip inside her mouth.

I saw that expression a lot.

Because we always sat on the bench and she always asked me about such things, *what do you remember from your childhood, what happened with that job you applied for, how do you think we should do this?*

I knew how. I wanted to go to the movies with her and for walks around Lake Sognsvann with her, I wanted everyone to see that stomach and see me and understand that it was mine, I was so childish, but she wanted something else entirely.

Just to meet on the bench.

Just talk and talk and plan.

Again and again, I rang the doorbell, and waited there and the little girls with the Chinese jump rope started saying hello to me and then Live came out with that serious gaze of hers, and sat down, and asked about something, *so what are your plans for the future?*

'Maybe we could do something one evening?' I said once. 'Go to the movies or something?'

It was late summer by then. A man walked past us wearing a boiler suit and a cap on backwards.

'That's the caretaker,' she said.

He twisted the spigot on the wall. Water started guzzling through a sprinkler.

Then she said: 'We both have our own lives. We have to continue with that.'

'But we are going to have a child together,' I said. 'It will be different then.'

She looked down, she picked small pieces of paint off the bench. But finally she peered up at me through her hair and said: 'You're right about that.'

'Thank you,' I said.

'But I don't have the energy for any kind of boyfriend stuff right now,' she said.

'Of course not,' I said. 'That's not what I meant.'

And I wanted to be somebody else, somebody who suited her, but she wouldn't let me and sometimes I felt like she was a jellyfish, she kind of slipped away from me and other times I felt like I was a dog on a leash, I wanted to come closer, I wanted to get inside, but there was always something or other that jerked me away and I had to shuffle home again, and then I had a beer and sat on the fire escape, the air smelt of exhaust fumes and the traffic drowned out everything, but it didn't matter because I got tipsy and I dreamt.

It was a long way from my dreams to my life at that time.

I dreamt of how I would grill steaks in her kitchen. Read her books. Paint the baby's room blue, lie in her bed and look at Saturn, listen to her say *I think the rings are fascinating.*

And I dreamt about giving her things. Trips to southern Europe, dresses, restaurant dinners and I would give her money for the child. Most of all.

I sat on that mini-balcony and the sun went down behind the blocks of flats and the clouds grew thin and dark red. What I wanted to do was to hand her the banknotes and say *here, don't you need a little for a pram?*

How stupid can you possibly be.

So I got hold of the money.

I put it in my back pocket, I walked through the city and reached her building. It was September but the asphalt was hot and I was just wearing a singlet. Outside the entrance the caretaker was painting the bench white, he was squatting down with a brush in his hand and his cap on backwards and sweating. I walked past him and pressed the doorbell.

'It's me,' I said.

'Come in,' she said.

I hadn't expected that, because usually she said *just a second, I'll be right down*, but now the lock buzzed and I walked up the stairs and there was a spring in my step, the sun shone through the windows on each landing and I imagined how we would sit in her kitchen again, and look at each other for a long time again and how I would hand her the money. In the stairway a window was open and I heard somebody singing outside, *Summertime and the living is easy*, I took the stairs four at a time and at the top I pushed down the door handle. But it was locked.

After a long while she opened it. The hallway was dark. She was just wearing her bathrobe. I leaned forwards and gave her a kiss on the cheek, there was something sticky and strong smelling in her hair.

'Sorry,' she said. 'I've got a hair mask on, you see.'

'Okay,' I said.

'Your hair gets a bit ugly when you're pregnant,' she said.

'I haven't noticed that,' I said.

'Thank you,' she said.

She looked at me, she waited for me to say something. But I wanted to go inside. I was so close, I was so childish. I didn't say anything.

'Can we do this here?' she said. 'It's a bit of a mess in here now.'

I knew that was a lie. But she stood there in front of me wearing just her bathrobe, I couldn't force my way past. So then I stuck my hand in my back pocket and pulled out the money and said what I had planned to say.

'Here's twenty thousand for you,' I said. 'Don't you need a little for a pram?'

'Twenty thousand?' she said.

'Yes,' I said. 'I haven't exactly helped out much financially. So far.'

But she just looked at the money, she didn't take it. And it was dark behind her, I couldn't understand why she didn't turn on the lights. And it was cold in the stairway, it gave me goose pimples.

'We were going to collaborate,' I said. 'We agreed about that.'

'But,' she said. 'You can't just give me twenty thousand?'

'Sure I can,' I said.

I heard a door opening, somebody ran down the stairs, the front door slammed.

'But,' she whispered. 'In cash?'

'Yes,' I said.

'Did you find a job then?' she said.

'I've had some odd jobs,' I said. 'You must need a little extra now.'

But she didn't take the money.

'Don't you want it?' I asked.

'Yes,' she said.

But I saw that she was about to start crying. In the dark, in the hallway, with her hair all wet and sticky. And I saw why. Why she had to cry.

Because I understood so little.

Because I could find a way to believe that somebody like her would be happy to receive twenty thousand in cash from somebody like me.

She took a step towards me.

'Thank you,' she said.

She reached out her hand.

'You're welcome,' I said.

So I got rid of that money, but I did it because she felt sorry for me, I had been so damn stupid, I turned around and walked down the stairs and I reached the first landing and looked up and she was still standing there.

She looked down at me and I looked up at her.

'Aren't you going inside?' I asked.

'Yes,' she answered.

'You mustn't catch a cold,' I said. 'Your hair is wet.'

'Yes,' she said. 'I'm being careful. I'm going inside now.'

'Talk to you soon,' I said.

'Thomas,' she said. 'Thank you for the money.'

And then I left, quickly, I reached the ground floor and twisted the lock around and shoved the door open and I wanted to get away, but I held onto the door. I stood there. One of the little girls was outside, silent, standing with her back to me, she had the Chinese jump rope wrapped around her hand because the bench had just been repainted. Everything was wrong.

And then it was just like somebody turned my body around. Turned me around.

I went inside again and the door closed behind me. I had a feeling. Like a fish hook, something that was tugging my heart upwards.

So I just walked, straight up, it smelt of cold concrete and somebody sang 'Summertime', everything was the same, everything was different, and then I was at the top and her door was ajar and I pulled it open all the way and there she stood, crying in the darkness and holding the banknotes in her hand and I said *but sweetheart*, and she said *where did the money come from, where did this money come from*, and I got dizzy and said *don't worry about it, you don't need to take it*, and she lifted a head made of porcelain that was on the sideboard, the head was hollow, *I'll put it here*, she said, *I don't want to spend it*, she pushed the money inside the porcelain head, *fine*, I said, *I've already bought a pram*, she said, *I bought one second-hand*, and then she started sobbing and then I could hold her, I kissed her and she kissed me and rubbed off her tears against my singlet, then I led her into the bathroom, I washed the dumb hair mask out of her hair, she sat on her knees and bent over the bathtub and the water ran over my hands. Then I turned off the shower and patted her neck and stuck my hand inside her bathrobe and felt her stomach and the sash slid open, then she got to her feet and we went into the bedroom and I looked at her back and at Saturn, I remembered what she'd said, *I think the rings are fascinating*, and then she came and then I came and when I left, I lifted the porcelain head and took the money with me, *I'll take this back to where it came from*, I said and she smiled then and that was the last time she smiled like that.

On the 18th of September that happened. And the entire autumn I waited for it to happen again.

But she was transformed.

She was just pregnant and her gaze was distant, she never asked to meet on the bench any longer and when I called, she just said *can we do it next week*.

That's how the autumn went. That's how the winter went. And on 14th March my phone rang. It was her girlfriend.

'Congratulations, Thomas,' she said. 'Your son was born.'

So he was born.

I entered the room. Live was lying in bed with her eyes closed. Water from melting snow dripped past the window, her girlfriend was sleeping in a beanbag chair by the wall, she looked exhausted, too. Then the door closed behind me, and Live opened her eyes and said: 'Hi. He's over here.'

I walked around her bed. There he was.

He looked like a little bird. He lay in that box made of Plexiglas. When he breathed it made a wheezing sound.

Then he opened his eyes.

'He opened his eyes,' I whispered.

'Yes,' Live said. 'He's been asleep for a long time.'

I stared.

Then he smiled.

'He's smiling,' I said.

Live smiled as well.

'No,' she said. 'He can't smile yet.'

'But he just did,' I said. 'He has dimples.'

'Did he?' she said.

She tried to sit up, but couldn't manage it, she moaned.

'I'll help you,' I said.

I cranked up the back of the bed.

She leaned to one side to look.

But he didn't smile any more. He kept his eyes closed and his eyelids trembled.

'He's dreaming,' she said.

'Is he?' I said.

'Yes,' she said. 'You can tell from the eye movements.'

Then I heard the beanbag chair rustle. It was her girlfriend waking up, she blinked and pulled down her sweater and looked at me.

'Congratulations again,' she said. 'Lovely little boy.'

She put on her glasses. I recognized her then, it was one of the women from the karaoke night.

'He has dimples,' I said.

'Does he?' she said.

'Yes,' I said. 'He smiled at me.'

Then she stood up and smoothed out her hair with her hands.

'They don't smile when they're this young,' she said. 'Maybe he had a bit of a stomach ache.'

So, suddenly he was born. Suddenly he could sit up, suddenly he could walk. Suddenly he could read, *L*, he said, *that's the letter for me and Mummy.* And I tried to follow along, but I wasn't really needed, because Live knew everything and I was clueless, she tested the bathwater with her elbow and cleaned his pacifier by sucking on it, she wrote his name on tags inside all his clothes and I was supposed to have him on visits, we signed papers, but I never found any proper job, and I never managed to fix up my flat nicely, I wanted to, but it just didn't happen, so there were no visits, and some evenings I became bitter, because what was the point of pulling it together when it didn't help, and other evenings I got drunk and called them and told them I loved them, and some days I forgot about them and other days I remembered them and then I went over there, I never called first, but Live was never angry, she just talked over the intercom and said *just a second, we'll come down.*

Then I could take a stroll with him through the city.

I gave him helium balloons and sneakers with flashing lights and policewomen smiled at me when I had him on my shoulders. I tied the string of the balloon tightly around his wrist and he stared up into the air.

But the differences just became greater.

Because everything I gave him was shiny and blinking and everything she gave him looked old fashioned, hand-knitted sweaters, rucksacks with a fox logo on them, and the time passed like that, several years passed like that.

They managed on their own.

So I carried on with my things.

And finally things have consequences, that's what my father always said and he was right.

*

Here comes Vibeke. She put lipstick on, it's pink.

She sits down beside me, she looks at me with that slow gaze and there's so much to think about, life and Live, and now I reach out my hand and rub my thumb up and down Vibeke's shoulder and she is surprised, but she smiles, it's been a long time since I've touched skin like that, it's been a long time since I have felt such thin straps and I say: 'It's nice to see you, Vibeke.'

'Likewise,' she replies and twists towards the bar and the bartender comes and says *yes my lady*, and she leans forwards and flirts with him and I know why, but it's too simple, I look at her watch, but can't see what time it is and then she turns to face me.

'You were going to tell me,' she says.

'Yes,' I say.

'Tell me about prison,' she says.

Her eyes are shiny.

'I learnt a lot in prison,' I say. 'I saw a psychologist.'

'Why's that?' she asks.

'Because I lost it,' I answer.

'Really?' she says. 'Tell me about that.'

Yes. It's true. I thought I would go under in the dark water, and now I tell Vibeke, I don't know if she understands, but she rests her chin on her hands and stares at me and I tell her, *it felt completely dark*, I say, and the water rose and rose, until that day, when we sat around the table and it was dinnertime, the others had stopped trying to talk to me by then. I sat and looked down into my fish au gratin. My thoughts were fucked up at that time, I thought about shapes and water and light and darkness, things that it's not possible to talk about.

Then the prison officer stood in the doorway.

'Kristiansen,' he said. 'There's a phone call for you.'

I put down my fork.

'Who is it?' I asked.

'I don't know,' he answered. 'The security guard patched it through.'

I looked at him.

'I think it's your girlfriend,' he said.

And I stood up. I followed behind him. I still don't understand how she had managed to get a call through, but she is, after all, one of those people, who makes directors listen and then we reached the telephone in the hallway, the receiver was dangling on the cord. I pulled it up and the prison officer leaned against the other wall.

'Hello,' I said.

'It's Live,' she said.

My hands started shaking then.

I didn't understand what I was supposed to do. I hadn't said goodbye to Leon, I didn't manage it during our trip to the cottage and then I left and Live had to fix it by herself, come up with a lie, she's such a good mother and I was a shit father and I'd heard the other guys, I knew what she was going to say, that now it was all over, now he was going to have another daddy, now she would give up on me once and for all.

'Why are you calling?' I asked.

The prison officer turned away.

'I wondered if we could come and visit you,' Live said. 'Can you get them to send us one of those visitors' permits?'

Then things got shuffled around in my head. First one way. Then the other.

'No,' I said.

'Why not?' she said.

'Just. No,' I said.

She didn't say anything.

'You have to walk through a metal detector,' I said.

'That doesn't make any difference,' she said. 'He needs to see his father.'

But it was impossible. Leon walking in there, where there's the rattling of keys in the hallways, where children have to walk through metal detectors and German shepherds sniff at them and the water rises gloomily every evening, Leon sitting on that kind of couch, where rapists have sex with their girl-friends and the closet is full of sheets and condoms, it was impossible.

'Never,' I said. 'Never come here with him.'

It was silent on the line then. I couldn't hear whether she had hung up.

'Hello?' I said.

'Yes, hello,' she said.

Then she was silent again. The prison officer pointed at his watch.

'And I don't want him to know where I am,' I said. 'Can't you just tell him I went on a trip?'

She didn't answer.

'Did you tell him already?' I asked.

Then I understood that she had. And the prison officer nodded towards the kitchen, but I couldn't hang up, I couldn't go back to the fish au gratin then, so I just turned my face towards the wall, and I guess the prison officer understood something or other, he let me stand there.

'So you've told him where I am?' I asked.

'I had to,' she answered.

'But did you tell him what I did as well?' I asked.

'No,' she answered.

'But are you going to tell him?' I asked.

'I thought I would say it in a nice way,' she answered.

But there are some things that can't be said in a nice way, so I slid down to the floor and tore at the neckline of my T-shirt and the prison officer came towards me, but I stared up at him and said *this is private*, and into the receiver I said *Live, do you want to destroy your child*, and I started talking fast, I held the receiver with both hands and I said something about how when you fight, then you fight and when there's asphalt beneath you, it gets ugly fast, I just babbled, I said something about water that was rising, because I hadn't talked to anyone for many weeks, and in the end I said: 'Tell him it was a crime of profit, at least.'

'Crime of profit?' she said.

'Yes, tell him it wasn't violence or anything like that,' I said.

'But Thomas,' she said. 'Leon doesn't know the difference.'

A strange sound came out when I breathed, and the prison officer lay his hand on my shoulder, but I shook him off and babbled on about how my motive was financial and the defence attorney was recently separated, and Live just listened, but finally she said: 'Thomas, Thomas, you're losing it. Isn't there a psychologist or someone in there you can talk to?'

'What?' I said.

'I think you should see a psychologist,' she said. 'It would be good for you and me and Leon and all of us.'

Then the conversation was over. She hung up and I got to my feet. I put the receiver back on the phone.

I brushed off my sweatpants.

The prison officer started walking and I walked behind him, the hallway was long and green, but when we reached the kitchen door, he turned around and said: 'Are you OK?'

Then I just answered: 'Maybe I should see a psychologist, actually.'

And he looked at me and my ripped T-shirt and said: 'Maybe that would be a good idea. I'll pass it on.'

And just two days later, I had a session.

So then life changed again.

Now Vibeke is smiling. She lifts her hand.

'Oh,' she says. 'That was a nice story.'

Then she strokes my cheek.

And then she leans towards me, she lays her head on my shoulder, her cheek is soft and I have never been able to resist softness, and her hair is nice, it's darkest furthest in, she lifts her head off my shoulder and peeks up.

'But honestly,' she says. 'You remember that I danced with you at the school formal?'

'Yes,' I say.

'I wore that velvet dress with one of those open backs, you kept putting your hands inside the dress,' she says.

And I think I remember something about something velvet, or that everything becomes velvet now, so I nod, and what was crumpled is smoothed out, I close my eyes for a moment, then she starts to laugh, and I open my eyes and I laugh too, and the bartender smiles, he wipes the counter with a rag and looks at us.

'You drink so fast,' Vibeke says. 'I've never seen anyone drink so fast. And it was nice to see you smile, too.'

She laughs again, and now I see.

I have drunk up the beer.

And this makes sense.

Because this is how I am.

And this is how I drink, quickly, so I order one more, and I say *of course I remember that dress, if there's one dress I won't forget, it's that one*, then she pats me on the cheek again, and then the beer comes and then evening comes, then the world starts to get black and red, it's been fourteen months since I last had a drink and now it affects me quickly, now it affects me nicely, and her shoulders are naked and I put my arm around her, but I can't forget Live, but she didn't want me, it was as simple as that.

'I had a lady who didn't want me,' I say.

'Don't you think I've had men who didn't want me?' Vibeke says. 'Now we're thinking about the future.'

And she's right about that, and I say she's wise, I tell her about the future, about Leon, *he can read,* I say, *he has dimples, he's so sensitive, he can't fall asleep without a pillow,* I tell her that a woman refused to let me buy him a pillow today.

'Refused?' Vibeke asks.

'Yes,' I answer.

Then she laughs and the heart on her tooth sparkles. I open my wallet, she gets to see Leon, and we lean towards each other, our heads touch.

Now everything makes sense. Now everything is fine. And people come down the stairs and brush snow off their jackets and say *how about that weather,* and Vibeke entwines her legs with mine, I remember alcohol now, I remember how it suits me, and Vibeke nods and Vibeke drinks and Vibeke looks at me.

'I like that you're honest,' she says.

'Thanks,' I say.

'My shout. Because you're so honest,' she says and the bartender stands over there and she turns around and holds up two fingers and turns towards me again, I like how she turns around, twists around, and how her eyes look at me, like hot water.

'So what are your plans for the evening?' she asks. 'For the rest of the evening?'

Her breath is warm.

'I have my son tonight,' I answer.

The bartender holds the glass under the tap, his bangs fall over his eyes. I like precisely this moment.

'Tonight?' Vibeke says.

I watch how the glass fills up.

'Six o'clock,' I say.

'But six o'clock *tonight*?' Vibeke says, she's speaking loudly now, I have to look at her, she looks at her watch and at me and at her watch again, and that watch, it looks like a little girl's watch, but she had that velvet dress once, and me, I wore blue jeans to a formal, I was another person then and everything was possible, the bartender comes with two pints, and I want everything to be possible still, but she gets up now, she says: 'He's not having any beer. He has his son starting at six o'clock this evening.'

The bartender puts the glasses down by the till. He looks at his watch.

'Put on your jacket,' Vibeke says.

Their eyes are different now.

Then my throat begins to pound, I can't handle that they're looking at me like that.

'I can't,' I say.

'What?' Vibeke says.

'I can't have him tonight after all,' I say.

'Why do you say that?' Vibeke says.

'I don't have everything ready,' I say.

'What is it that you don't have?' she asks.

'A pillow,' I say. 'I told you. There was a woman who refused to help me.'

And then Vibeke opens her mouth, she stares at me, *but good Lord, was that because he's spending the night with you tonight*, she says, *but oh my God, he doesn't give a shit about pillows*, and I try to explain that he does and the bartender turns away and I lean over the bar, towards the beer, but then she takes hold of my wrist and holds on tight to my arm and says: 'Do you want me to buy a pillow and come to your place?'

The bartender bends over, he starts emptying the dishwasher.

'Will you pull yourself together if I buy a pillow?' Vibeke asks.

The bartender turns towards us. He has his hands full of glasses.

'Vibeke,' he says. 'It's ten past.'

'But he lives just right up the street,' Vibeke says.

Then he smiles and puts the clean glasses on the bar.

'Haven't you tried to change people before?' he says.

Then he shakes his head.

And then there is something or other that gets me onto my feet.

I stand up.

'Are you pulling yourself together?' Vibeke asks.

Because people change all the time. And me, I'm changing now.

Now I take my jacket. I nod.

And then I turn around and run.

*

I shove the door open. It's snowing. And my shoes slip on the snow and the red light on the clock above the intersection is illuminated, I should have been home now and I start up the hill and my breathing smarts because I couldn't be bothered to do any cardio when I was inside, and there's a ringing sound, a bus stops and lets people off, they are in my way, I push them aside, but the ringing sound, it comes after me, it's my phone, but it's new and nobody has the number and then it stops and I'm out of breath already and what's the point of changing if you can't make it home by six o'clock, when you're not going to make it anyway, and now the people are gone and the pavement is slippery and I get snow on my face and the phone rings again, but nobody has my number.

Yes.

Live has my number.

I stop.

I pull my phone up out of my pocket and it has to be Live and it's Live.

I press the button.

'Hi,' I say.

I look for something to lean against.

'Hi,' she says. 'Are you running?'

'No,' I say.

'Oh,' she says.

I walk a few steps more, I lean against a lamp post.

'Are you outside?' she asks. 'I can hear cars?'

'No, no,' I say. 'I'm just standing on the balcony and smoking a cigarette.'

I move all the way up against the post. I lean my forehead against the metal and close my eyes and take a deep breath and try to release it without making a sound.

'Well, anyway,' Live says. 'I'm very sorry about this, but you see how the weather is, there are tailbacks everywhere. I almost didn't make it to the kindergarten in time.'

'Yes,' I answer.

I don't really understand what she is saying.

'Yes, sorry,' Live says. 'It's such a shame since it's the first time. I know you were looking forward to it.'

And now I think I understand what she's saying.

They're not coming.

I open my eyes. I look around.

'So you're not coming?' I ask and yellow light glows from the windows in the blocks of flats and people walk past me on all sides, they have huge bags and prams in their hands.

I stand still.

'Wait a minute, I just have to fix the hands-free,' Live says, I hear a clicking sound from her phone and I stand still and the snow falls onto my shoes, but now Live is back again and she says: 'Yes, what was I going to say. Oh yes, we're in the car, Leon is looking forward to it and everything. But we're half an hour late or something. I called you four times, didn't you hear the phone?'

I look up. The snow is falling so quickly through the lamplight, huge flakes against my eyes. I look towards the intersection. Vibeke is standing beneath that little overhang. She has put on her knitted jacket, she is looking at me.

'Just come when you can,' I say.

'Fine,' Live says.

'Thank you very much,' I say.

'You don't need to thank me,' Live says. 'He's your own son.'

She says goodbye.

I put the phone in my pocket.

Then I bend over and pick some snow up from the pavement and put it in my mouth and spit it out again. I take more snow and rub my face and neck, because everything has to be clean now, completely clean, completely new and my hands grow cold from the snow and I straighten up and look down at Vibeke, I'm clean now, new, and she stands in front of the pub and I wave at her.

She smiles.

I wave with my whole arm.

'Thanks!' I shout.

Vibeke nods. She ties the belt of the jacket around her waist. Then she points towards the pillow shop, and then she turns around and leaves.

Now is when we run away. We are standing between the buildings. I tell the kids to take off their rucksacks.

'Why?' Mia asks.

She's wearing a quilted parka and her back is to the sun. That hair of hers is far too red.

'Because you must listen to your big sister,' I say.

Mikael pulls off his rucksack and gives it to me.

'You too,' I say to Mia. 'Give me your rucksack.'

But she just stares, and we don't have time for this. I turn away from them and push my way between the dustbins for paper. It's dark here, I blink hard and then I see our plastic bags, I pull them out and bring them with me into the light. There is frost on the asphalt.

'Are those our things?' Mia asks.

'Take off your rucksack,' I say.

Nobody can see us here. Nobody from school and nobody from day care, but all the same my pulse is hammering, it's hammering rapidly. Because somebody might come by, somebody might be standing at the window in a building and people remember me, they always do, *you have charisma*, Cecilie said, but it's dangerous now, because it's true, old ladies remember me and all the teachers, everyone who works in a shop and the kind of people who watch from behind curtains, I can't do a bloody thing without people staring and remembering everything I do.

'Mia,' I say. 'We're just waiting for you, now.'

She pulls off her rucksack, slowly. Then she drops it right on the ground. But I don't have time to yell, I just turn it over and shake everything out.

'But the books!' Mia says.

I open Mikael's rucksack and turn it upside down as well, I shake the things out, the juice bottle and the Spiderman lunchbox, two rolled-up drawings and there is the boat pen he got from his father.

Then I pick up Mia's schoolbooks from the ground and open the hatch in the dustbin and push the books inside.

'What?' Mia says.

I bend over again and pick up the homework folder and pencil case. I lift the hatch and push everything through the opening, Mikael's drawings and the juice bottle, the lunchbox, I push it all in, then I take the plastic bags full of clothing and put them into the rucksacks and pick up the boat pen and give it to Mikael.

But now he has that look.

And I don't like it.

He has those frightened eyes.

And I can't bear it that my brother's eyes are like that, because I have wondered about this, about whether fear grows with the body, like other scars, like our mother's caesarean section, when she got fatter, the scar just grew larger.

I pat his head through his cap.

'I'll explain later,' I say. 'We just have to catch a bus. Is that OK?'

He nods.

'Fine,' I say. 'Now let's put on the rucksacks.'

They put on their rucksacks.

I stand behind Mia, I lift up her hair and braid it quickly, I put the braid down into her jacket and pull the hood over her head.

Then I take hold of their hands and start walking. Between the buildings and down to the city centre.

Now is when we run away. Now is when it happens.

The sun shines against the ice on the asphalt.

The sky is light blue and clear.

*

'Where are we going?' Mia asks.

I am sitting between them. We have the entire back seat to ourselves.

'It's a surprise,' I say.

Mia sighs and leans her forehead against the window. A bus backs out from the platform beside us. Mikael turns his pen upside down, the Danish Cruise Ship slides downward inside it.

And now finally the bus starts, the seat shakes, I take off my hat. Mikael turns the pen over again, the Danish Cruise Ship slides backwards into place.

'Why can't you just say it?' Mia asks.

'Because you have to trust me,' I answer.

Because I don't trust her. She isn't suspicious enough, she talks to people and thinks they can help, I've seen it, ever since she was small, she sat on the laps of her kindergarten teachers and fiddled with their hair, she held the hands of strange fathers and asked to go home with friends. But I know how people are. They lie there like logs, like the crocodiles on the Animal Planet. And I know what it will say in the newspaper. *Last seen near Toyen School, a one p.m. yesterday, the sisters are ethnic Norwegian, the little brother is of Norwegian-Moroccan origin.* And the pictures of us will be on the front page, Mia with a pencil in her hand and her hair red and curly over her shoulders, *the siblings are seventeen, seven and four years old,* and the police will interview Faiza at the after-school care programme and at the day-care centre they will stay in the changing room for a long time, lifting garment after garment from Mikael's place and say *can you tell if something is missing here, was there something unusual about Mikael on Tuesday, can you remember what Rebekka said when she picked him up?*

But they can just forget about it.

They can just forget about us.

Because now the bus is backing out. Now it's turning, now we're driving away, we're driving away now, now the barrier is going up and we are sitting way in the back as I planned and I paid in cash as I planned, and I hid Mia's hair, and I didn't look the driver in the eyes, because I know how people are

found, all the girls, they ask for help, they look people in the eyes and use their mobiles and take taxis
or go around wearing short-shorts and faces of
desperation, in the middle of the night, so everyone
can see.

But not me.

Because my rucksack is full of food and the kids'
rucksacks are full of clothing and the key is hanging
on the bird feeder and I just have to smile, I have
planned everything, I put my arms around the kids
and give them a tight squeeze. Then I look out the
window.

Taxi drivers who are leaning against the roofs of
their cars. A roundabout, a tunnel and then we're out
of the tunnel, then there aren't any people, just cars
and now the road is big and wide and there is the
ocean.

'Hello,' the driver says over the loudspeaker.

I jump.

'Welcome to the Valdres express,' he says.

'Valdres,' Mia says.

She's so sharp. Cecilie said so too. *That one
thinks clearly*, Cecilie said, that was in June, Cecilie
went with me after school and picked them up, she
held both of them by the hand, they hopped from
one foot to the other at her side and Mia talked the
entire time, *Cecilie, are you going to have dinner*

with us? Cecilie, do you have brown eyes, do you have a father, have you been on a camping trip, Cecilie, is God the same as Allah?

The driver stops talking. Mia turns towards me.

'You said that afterwards you would explain,' she says.

I nod.

'It's afterwards now,' she says.

'Lower your voice,' I say.

'Is someone trying to catch us?' Mikael says.

'No,' I say. 'They don't understand where we are.'

'Where are we then?' Mia says.

'We're on the bus,' I say.

'But where's the bus going?' Mia says.

She never gives up. Just asks and asks, until she gets a headache, that's how she is, she never quits. But I know what I have to do then.

'To a secret place,' I say. 'But I can tell you what it's like there.'

Then I start talking. Softly, in a fairy-tale voice.

'It's a place where you have never been,' I say.

Mikael pulls his legs up onto the seat. He lays his head in my lap. Mia looks at me. But I just look back at her. And finally she gives up, she sighs and curls up under the window.

'A brown cottage in a forest,' I say.

'What are we going to do there?' Mikael asks.

'There we are going to figure out . . . everything,' I say.

I keep telling the story until their eyes become shiny.

How the log walls will be thick. How silent trees will surround us on all sides, how Mia and Mikael will gather wood while I heat water in a pot.

'Why?' Mia asks.

'Because there everything is like in the old days,' I say.

I tell them about the water buckets. Mikael takes a lock of my hair and tickles his cheek with it. I tell them about the outhouse and the fireplace and how I will play the guitar in the evening and I remember those days, when I understood how everything is, that we are made for this: walking through the heather, getting water from a well. Turning on the radio. And I stood with the washing-up brush in my hand and stared at the radio. That such an old radio could play such new songs.

Now it's getting dark. At the very bottom of the sky the clouds are red.

I pull my fingers through Mikael's hair.

The logs in the fireplace, how they glow. And Cecilie crouching beside me, she smokes slowly and leans forward and blows the smoke up the chimney.

'Why don't you tell us more?' Mikael asks.

'I got distracted,' I say.

'Don't get distracted,' he says.

'And when we go to bed we have to put a screen in front of the fireplace,' I say. 'So the sparks don't fly out of the fire.'

But I was like an immigrant in that country. Because there were secrets about everything. Open the damper and shut off the gas, put a stone on the cover of the well.

'But whose cottage is it?' Mia asks.

'A friend's,' I say.

Mia sits up and turns towards the window.

'It's Cecilie's for sure,' she says.

There's a petrol station. We drive in towards it, huge hamburger signs are lit up, we stop in the back, the bus doors open. It smells like winter.

The people come in, there are many of them, there are women and I don't like women like this, I don't like gazes like this and those kinds of colourful scarves and one of them sits right in front of us, even though there are many empty seats, she takes a seat far too close to us.

'But what about school?' Mia says.

'Hush,' I say. 'It's fine.'

'But tomorrow's a school day,' Mia says.

'Close your eyes,' I say. 'Time to go to sleep.'

Mikael looks up from my lap. His eyes are black, they are Mehmet's eyes.

'It's daytime,' he says.

'You'll be staying up late,' I say.

Mia's freckles look dark. That's because she's pale and she has dark circles under her eyes, I can see it and me, too, I have it as well, *poor self-care abilities*, I see it every time I walk past a mirror.

'So that's why you have to sleep,' I say.

'Then you have to sing "The Wolf Song",' Mia says.

'Close your eyes,' I say.

'Yes, you have to sing,' Mikael says.

'I'll start when you've closed your eyes,' I say.

Mikael closes his eyes. And finally Mia does what I say. She sighs and leans into the corner and squeezes her eyes shut.

Then I sing for them.

In my softest voice.

> *The wolf howls in the dying light*
> *He's hungry and cannot sleep*
> *His den is dark in the winter night*
> *The woods are silent and deep*
>
> *Oh wolf, oh wolf, do not come near*
> *You'll never have my child.*

*

Now the lights are glittering. Now the darkness comes.

Now they fall asleep. Mia in the corner and Mikael with his head in my lap.

Then I start to tremble.

But I know what it is, it's not dangerous, it's just the body's logic. I look at my hand, it's in Mikael's hair and it's shaking, but it's only logical, it's just delayed, because these are the hands that found the letter, I was standing by the kitchen table and looking through the mail, there were bills and an advertisement from a sporting goods store and then the letter was lying there, in the middle of the pile, I saw Mum's name, I saw the logo, these are the hands that picked up the envelope.

Then I went into my bedroom. I locked the door, I sat on the bed. I held the letter in my hands. Now they are shaking.

Because I know about letters like this. I already know, I can't be fooled. So I opened the envelope.

And now my head starts pounding. From the way they write, I know very well how it turned out, but they write about it in a way that makes it sound different, but now my brain is not my brain, it's like an animal now, and I don't like it, because I have to think clearly, I have to think like Cecilie said, *your mind is so logical*. But what if they put a missing persons alert for us on the radio? What if the bus driver heard it? And I know what he'll do then, but this,

this isn't logic, this is my imagination. But imagine if he has heard us and calls somebody and says *I have two children and a young girl here you should check out*, and I know what will happen then, I will be swept aside, because that's how the system is, *her own needs must be put first*, and if you get up and leave, that's just one more thing they write down, *struggles with impulse control, little willingness to collaborate*, but I know what will happen if I disappear, Mia and Mikael will become completely silent and then they'll become drug addicts and now my hands get hot, they get large, now I want to get rid of something or throw up, but I can't, because I have to sit here quietly, and this is all just my imagination, it is, but it's true that the letter came, it was lying there, and it's true that it was my fault, but that's the past, that there is the past and I have to think of the future now, but then I must do something, because there is poison running through my body now and my thoughts are destroyed by it, I can't sit still.

I move Mikael and stand up.

I walk right past the women to the middle of the bus. I pull a plastic cup out of the machine and there's lemon powder in the bottom. I fill it with hot water and squeeze the cup with my hands, the tea burns through the plastic. It hurts. It feels good.

I walk back, I stare at the cup.

I burn myself the entire way.

I sit down and drink the tea. Then I get a little clearer and a little warmer.

I have a plan. I think logically.

I'm doing it now and I did it yesterday. I sat on the bed and put the letter back in the envelope, my thoughts were clicking like falling dominos. I knew what we had to do: run away. I knew what we needed: money. And I knew what I had to do: find Morten.

But first everything had to be as usual, so I picked up the kids and brought them home, I watched Mia do her homework, she spelt out *what* and *who* and my brain was just completely white, but the kids didn't notice anything, I sent them to the bathroom and pulled down the shades and sat on the edge of the bed and sang 'The Wolf Song', and then I said goodbye to Mum and went out, the streets were dark and the cars were white with frost, I knew where I was going, my legs took me there.

I opened the door to the pub. I saw him from behind, the black leather jacket and the ugly haircut, I am so glad that guy is not my father. I went over to the table where he was sitting. There was a football match on the telly, I had the letter in my inside pocket, his parting was slick; he uses way too much hair wax. I put my hand on his shoulder. He looked up and smiled. And stopped smiling when he realized it was me.

'Can I talk to you for a minute?' I said.

'Here?' he said.

'We can go over there,' I said.

I walked past the pinball machine. There I turned around. He stood up and followed me.

Then we went around the corner, to the hallway by the loo. It was darker there. The football match made a lot of noise, the people in the pub shouted *o-oh*, and then I said I had to borrow a thousand kroner.

'Why's that?' Morten asked.

He put his hand on his breast pocket, that's where he had his wallet.

'We need it,' I said.

'But for what?' he asked.

Then everyone was screaming, on the telly and in the pub, a man roared and a chair scraped and tipped over, but I just stared at Morten.

'It's not that I'm a cheapskate, Rebekka,' he said. 'But you know that if I forked out every time your mum said she needed something, there'd be no end to it.'

He smiled. I don't like people smiling when they are speaking ill of Mum.

'It's not Mum whose asking,' I said. 'You can see that it's me here.'

'I see that,' he said. 'But you know I pay child support for Mia every month.'

'You know I wouldn't ask if I didn't have to,' I said.

'But it's not the first time that . . . ' he said.

Then I leaned in towards his face. So my charisma would work. He smelt of hair wax and beer, I held him by the shoulders, the whites of his eyes were yellow, and he didn't know what happened, I had to have this money. And I don't know why he got scared, but he did, people do. He took out his wallet.

'A thousand kroner will do,' I said and he stared down into his wallet, he looks completely idiotic when he holds things so close to his eyes.

He pulled out two 500-kroner notes.

'Thanks,' I said. 'We're lucky to have you.'

I folded the bills and put them in the pocket of my trousers.

And I know what's going to happen. He's the first one the police are going to talk to. It doesn't matter, he's so dumb that he's got nothing to say.

But still, I hate him. He is the one I hate the most and the most frequently.

Even though Mehmet gets into fights when he's out drinking and has friends who laugh and speak Arabic and look at me, Morten is the one I hate. Because of the furniture he assembles in our house and how it is at his place, the kitchen with tiles above the sink, and that lady who makes lasagne and tacos and hangs up photographs from their trips to the Mediterranean in the hallway, and that bloody apprenticeship certificate of his, on the wall in a frame, but his new kids are such mouth-breathers, can't he just blow their noses from time to time, and I hate how he comes to our place and parks the car on the sidewalk so everyone will see it and carries in flat cardboard boxes and Mia and Mikael stare while he assembles desks and sideboards and idiotic stools, we don't need stools, so why does he give them to us, and then he leaves again. And I know how he talks at the pub afterwards. *I brought along a stool for the little guy, too*, that's the kind of thing he says, and the pinball machine flashes and the ladies tilt their heads and say *it's a good thing they have someone like you who's so resourceful*.

But have they forgotten about her?

Have they forgotten about Mum, how she was, how she really is? The way she was when I was little, how she and Dad and I walked through the Botanical Gardens and they each held one of my hands and Dad sang.

Oh, give me land, lots of land under starry skies above
Don't fence me in.
Let me ride through the wide open country that I love
Don't fence me in.

They held me by my hands and threw me forward, I flew many metres with each step, I was wearing the red coat that floated behind me, *let me wander over yonder till I see the mountains rise*, Dad sang, and when we reached the outdoor cafe, Mum stood behind his chair and slowly stroked his hair. But they don't remember that. And she read all the books in the bookshelf, she sat on the couch completely still and read them and I sat between her feet then, with a book about outer space which she'd borrowed for me from the library, she always knew what I wanted, and don't they remember how she arranged an autumn party for the neighbourhood, then she made balloon lanterns with tea lights inside and they were of tissue paper and flew towards the sky, they don't remember how she lit the Christmas tree and served mulled wine from a huge pot, because Mum, she's so happy when she's happy, and sometimes she's still like that, but then it's too much, she gets into the Christmas spirit and gives everyone at the pub a present, afterwards they go arm in arm to an after-party, all of them and she forces them to sing 'Silent Night' and once they're singing, she sings the harmony, she sings well, but they laugh when she's not looking, and Morten, he brought her home with him that one time and he must understand that no matter what, he should thank her for ever after, because she was the one who gave him Mia.

Mia sleeps with such concentration. She doesn't need to squeeze her eyes like that. I lean to one side and place my hand on her forehead and smooth out that wrinkle.

I see my reflection in the windowpane.

And I just don't understand. That that's me. Because I have changed so much. In one single year, just one year ago I was the way I had always been, I'd just started upper secondary school, I just sat in the classroom and looked out the window, at the gymnasium building, it was of brick, pigeons lived up on the roof and sometimes they flew in huge arcs over the schoolyard, those pigeons always did everything at the same time.

During the midday break people sat on the asphalt and played the guitar and wore half-finger gloves, because that was the kind of school it was, and I didn't have any friends, but I didn't care, because none of those people knew anything about me.

I walked out the gate and up along the river and looked at the leaves. I threw stones into the water and ate my bag lunch while I leaned my back against a bridge. I didn't dream. I just picked up the kids, got dressed in the morning and undressed in the evening. I just did what I was supposed to do, what I've always done.

Then Cecilie came.

I run my hand through Mikael's hair. It's warm underneath.

Then Cecilie came. Into French class.

She'd changed schools and suddenly she was sitting there, at the desk next to mine. She reached out her hand and said her name.

She spoke softly. I had never seen her before. But now I saw her. Every time I turned away from the window.

'Hey, you,' she said. 'Do you have that grammar book with all the verbs in the back?'

I blushed then, I could feel it, I don't know why, but I leaned over my rucksack and rummaged around down there until my face was no longer hot, then I pulled out the book and gave it to her.

And she didn't know anything about me. She just nodded and thanked me and bent over my book and afterwards she asked me if we could work together.

That's how my brain woke up.

Because I didn't know that language was like that. I hadn't thought about this business of past tense and present tense and gender and number correspondence, I hadn't understood that it was logical. But then I understood everything. She just read the rules out loud, *an indirect object comes before a direct object, je donne, je le donne, je te le donne,* and in every French class one light bulb after the next was switched on in my head.

The sunshine in through the window, the teacher who sat correcting something, and all the empty desks, because people just kept quitting and quitting that French class. But not us.

'Do you want to practise together today?' Cecilie said.

'Practise?' I said.

'After school,' Cecilie said.

'OK,' I said.

It was that spring. The pigeons just kept flying and I got such good grades suddenly, Bs and As and Bs again, my French quizzes were full of smiley faces, so I put them on the kitchen counter and Mum found them and leaned over them and said *what's this, my goodness*.

Because she sort of woke up too, she brightened, that's how we are, one for all, and on one of those days I walked through the shopping plaza and then I saw a note in the window of the bakery, which read: 'Full-time help wanted. You are: Service-minded. Conscientious. Independent'.

So I told Mum about it and she flipped a pork chop in the pan and answered *maybe the time has come*.

And the time had come. Because that's how we are. All for one.

She got the job. And three days a week I had French class and every day I had someone to talk to during break, someone to walk along the river with at lunch, and April came and I got such a desire to fix everything, I took a huge refuse bag into the bathroom and swept wisps of hair and toilet-paper rolls and Kleenexes with make-up on them into it. I sorted the pile of dirty laundry, I put the smallest garments in bags and carried them outside with me and threw them into a Salvation Army container, and when I came back, Mum patted my hand and said *you are a real neatnik, aren't you*, and her hand was cool. She was calm. Not sad and not afraid. She was ordinary.

She made it to work on time every day. I cleaned the refrigerator and threw out all the old rotten food and returned the empties and washed the floor underneath where they'd been, I rubbed away the sticky rings and Mum came home from work, she brought bread and currant buns for the kids, she dried off the counter and put the bread on the cutting board. And I thought: It's over now. She's done. With Dad and with death. Now we're done with it.

And on some Saturdays I put my old red coat on Mia and walked with the kids down to the shopping plaza. Mia hopped away, because she didn't want to step on cracks and the coat flew after her, I pushed open the door to the bakery, we sat by the window and watched Mum while she did everything she was supposed to do. And she did what she was supposed to do. She cleaned off the tables. She swept the floors. She winked at us and stacked clean plates at the end of the counter, and she liked to wash the floors with a mop, she liked serving coffee and saying *three for the price of two*, but I saw what she liked best, that was to ring up the prices and say the total, *fifty-nine fifty, please.*

And I was just happy. Happy when I went to school and happy when I left. Happy when I locked the door and happy when I unlocked it again, happy when I sang 'The Wolf Song' and when the flock of pigeons flew over the gymnasium and the sun reflected from underneath their wings, then I said *look over there* and Cecilie said *goodness, how pretty*. I went home again and put down my rucksack, the house was tidy and the dustbin emptied and the laundry hamper and the clotheshorse, and Mum said she could pick up the kids, but I replied *it's OK*, because I had so much energy and the kids came running towards me when I came to pick them up, Mia's face was filled with freckles and I made spaghetti bolognese and Mum said *well, my goodness, you've become such a good cook*, and every Thursday I took the train out of the city to practise 'my French.

Cecilie lived in a house with columns in front of the garage. The window frames were pink, she said *Mum's a little nuts, don't worry about how it looks here*.

So we sat on the floor of her bedroom, on the thick white carpet. We had books and Magic Markers and pencils that disappeared into the carpet all the time, we just wrote and read and understood things and on one of those days she looked up and said: 'You're a special person.'

'Oh,' I said.

'Have you thought about that?' she said.

'No,' I said.

'You are,' she said. 'You don't think like other people.'

But I knew. I should have known. There's a reason why I don't have friends like that.

But I just daydreamed.

I thought about love, then.

If I went to the store and saw a father teaching his son to ride a bicycle. Or old people who walked hand in hand through the city centre. All kinds of people were carrying on like this that spring, the fathers just ran and ran, gripping the bike carriers with their hands, I saw love everywhere. It was a delusion. Or else, it was true. I don't know for sure. And I remember one day, we had an end-of-term exam in Norwegian, but I played truant and lay under a huge tree in the Botanical Gardens and at two o'clock Cecilie came and sat down beside me and told me about the questions and hit me on the head with her notebook and said *you would have managed it easily*, I just lay in the grass and turned away, but then she stared at me and said *it's completely idiotic if you don't finish school.*

'Mm,' I said.

'Because you're really smart,' she said. 'You can be whatever you want to be.'

'I don't want to be anything in particular,' I said.

I just said it so she would keep talking. It was like being drawn, in art class, it tickled, and I wanted her to ask more, because I knew what I wanted, I knew exactly. How I would repeat some classes and just get As and start studying physics and get a job at the university, how I would have furniture of glass and steel and the kids would grow up and come to visit and I would serve them cake on a glass table and I would do research on the stars and the laws of nature, *it's the laws of nature people have confused with God*, Dad said, and I would work all the time and in my office the shelves would be full of thick books and the office would be on one of the top floors and at night I would sit there and point my astronomy telescope out the window.

I lay beneath the tree. The shadows moved across her face.

'I don't want to become anything in particular,' I repeated.

But then Cecilie leaned over me and stared at my stomach.

'But tan,' she said. 'You've at least become that.'

Mia mumbles something in her sleep. I lift Mikael's hair. It slides out of my hand, little by little, like a fan.

I see myself in the window again. That was the face Cecilie saw.

And actually that was what I couldn't stand. It's like with children, before they taste sweets, they don't know what they are, they don't know that it's what they want. Then they are given sugar and go crazy every Saturday because they have to have it. But I didn't know that. Everything is so messy, sometimes I just don't understand what life is up to. But I know what Dad would have said: *That's life, Rebekka. There's no system to it, it's just the carbon atom's chemistry.*

It's true. No system.

Because then it was June and then I showed her my things, we climbed over the fence around the Toyen swim centre, it was night time and the swimming pools rippled and flowed, we dove as quietly as we could and no night watchman came, no German shepherd, and afterwards we lay on towels in the dark and everything smelt of freshly cut grass and chlorine.

'Shall we go on holiday this summer?' Cecilie asked.

'What?' I said.

'Go on holiday,' she said.

'Yes,' I said.

She smiled then.

'To my cottage then, maybe?' Cecilie asked.

'Yes,' I said.

And I didn't think about the past. Or about Dad or death. Because my thoughts were like a telescope. And through the telescope I just saw one thing: her.

In the darkness at the Toyen swimming pool. In the light at the Botanical Gardens. We sat by the fish pond and threw pieces of hamburger buns to the fishes. We didn't get hungry. We didn't get thirsty. I wasn't worried about the kids.

'You seem so wise,' Cecilie said.

'Oh,' I said.

'Have you experienced a lot?' she said.

'I don't know,' I said. 'Maybe a little.'

Then the summer holiday came. Cecilie rang the doorbell and we walked through the city. My back was sweating under my rucksack. We walked to the bus station.

We sat on this bus.

I had this rucksack.

We drank this exact same lemon tea.

Mikael moves. The boat pen falls on the floor. I lean forward and pick it up and put it into his jacket pocket.

*

There's the church. With lights up along the wall. There's the turn.

Now I have to wake up the kids.

I nudge them.

Mia yawns. I take hold of Mikael and sit him up, his body is limp.

'We have to get off now,' I say. 'Put your coats on.'

I push the stop signal button on the ceiling.

Mikael closes his eyes and sinks down on the seat again, but he can't be this slow now, the bus is already pulling over on the side of the road. I stand up and support myself against the back of the seat in front of me, I pick up my rucksack.

'Come on,' I say.

The bus has stopped now, I can hear the doors opening.

Mikael tries to put on his jacket, but he's too tired.

'The zipper,' he says.

'We'll get dressed outside,' I say. 'Just get off.'

Then they stand up and stagger down the aisle, I gather the clothes and rucksacks in my arms and try to run towards the door, but this wasn't how we were supposed to do it, because the tins of food rattle in my rucksack and the women look at me, my scarf drags along the floor, I walk down the stairs, the air floods towards me, it's cold, it freezing cold.

Then I drop everything in a heap on the road.

This was not how we were supposed to do it. We were supposed to be just anybody. I am sure the driver is watching us in the mirror now, he's staring now. Because everything is supposed to be so right in order for everything to be right, your hair is supposed to be combed and the lunchboxes washed, their eyes are everywhere.

But then the bus starts up again.

Our breath turns into huge white clouds. The kids try to catch them with their hands, they laugh.

'Stop it now,' I say. 'Put this on.'

I open the rucksacks and pull out more clothes, I'm shaking, because the cold penetrates rapidly, further and further into my body, I pull quilted snow pants onto them and neck warmers, then I pull up the hoods and they look like two Eskimos. But now I am really shaking, I find my own clothes and pull them on, I wind the scarf around my neck.

I look down the road.

The woods are completely silent, with huge banks of snow along the road.

The bus is gone.

And then I am filled with such happiness.

I squat down and kiss them hard and quickly. Mia wrinkles her nose, it doesn't matter, I kiss her cheek again. The air is as cold as ice, it's kind of sparkling.

Then I lean back and look at them.

'Now it starts,' I say.

'What starts?' Mikael says.

'Our trip,' I say. 'Isn't it nice here?'

'Very,' Mikael says.

The air stings in my nose. I see Mikael's wrist, he's so thin, I pull the sleeve of his jacket down over the mitten.

Then I stand up and take hold of their hands and start walking.

The snow squeaks. I stop, the kids stop, too.

Then everything becomes quiet again.

And it's good and the sky is dotted with stars and here it's not like everyone is watching us. I notice it, no cars come, no people, I lead the kids along the road, the spruce trees here are so tall and pointy, it goes with the stars, and the houses look kind of closed, they are far away from the road.

This was where I wanted to go.

Now we're here.

And the kids are so pretty. I look down at them. I remember when they were born, they lay in a dark blue bag, I bent under the canopy and peeked, first there was Mia, her hair was red and the duvet's pattern was like a summer meadow and then, a few years later, it was Mikael who lay there, the duvet was faded, the blades of grass had become light green. But he was just as pretty, his eyes were open and black and as shiny as mirrors. And Mum, she was tired, I washed her hair while she sat on a stool in the shower, she said *you are my guardian angel.*

There's the intersection. The houses are closer together. But the windows are dark, and the store is closed, there is a large sign hanging on the wall that reads 'For Sale'. I like places like this. Then we take a right and the road begins to slope upwards. And I remember when we took a taxi here, when I saw mountains like this for the first time, they were blue then, they are white now, and the taxi driver stared at Cecilie in the rear-view mirror for the entire ride and asked if we would be alone up there. But she didn't answer, she just talked to me and pointed as we drove, *there's the waterfall, there's the tree line, that lake there is called Aurtjern.* Then we reached the turnaround, *here's our letter box,* and she smiled as she paid, we lifted out our bags, the taxi drove away, the gravel spraying out from beneath the tyres.

We stood before Aurtjern. And she said that we had to touch the boom barrier with both hands before we walked the final stretch, *then the summer holiday has started,* she said. She stood before the barrier and rested her hands on it. The wind was blowing a little, it moved the trees. Behind the boom barrier was the road we would take.

So I walked over to her and touched the barrier and the metal was warm beneath my hands.

'Can we walk a little more slowly?' Mia says.

I stop. She looks at the ground.

'Is there something wrong with you?' I ask.

'I just got a little hot on the bus,' she says.

I nod.

'And I have a little bit of a headache,' she says.

But that won't do. She can't have a headache now.

139

'It will pass soon, for sure,' I say.

A car comes towards us, white headlights, I stop and pull the kids to me, snow flies up from the tyres.

'We have to walk in a line,' I say. 'Because we're in the countryside now. There's no sidewalk in the countryside.'

I start walking again. Our shadows change along with the light from the streetlights, and I turn around and walk backwards for a bit. I like seeing them like this, Mikael first, Mia afterwards, we reach a streetlight, his face turns yellow, his eyelashes create long, black shadows.

'But around the cottage there aren't any cars at all,' I say.

'Oh,' Mikael says.

'Because everything is like in the old days there,' I say.

'Yes,' Mikael says.

I turn around and walk straight ahead again. And now I'm looking forward to it, I am looking forward to getting there, because I remember how it was, she unlocked the door and we walked in, the floorboards creaked under our feet, I put my rucksack on the floor. Everything was so calm there. Green chequered curtains. A bread box. At home such things are completely different, the curtains don't seem to hang as calmly. We were going to be there for one week and after just two days there were paths beaten down in the grass, from the cottage to the outhouse, to the shed, to the well. I got a kind of rhythm in my body.

And in the daytime we fixed things.

We put on old wool sweaters, I repaired a rain gutter, we carried wood from the shed and our sweaters got full of bark. Then we swam in Aurtjern and dried off in the sun, we walked home again with towels around our heads and afterwards it was evening, then we lay on the couch. Outside the forest was blue. And the fire flickered in the hearth and Cecilie sang old songs and played on an ancient guitar.

'It's only got five strings,' she said.

'That doesn't matter,' I said. 'You play really well.'

Then she started singing another song.

I once had a girl
or should I say
she once had me

I sat up and stared. Because it was that song. Dad sang that song. For Mum and me, I remembered it then, it was that exact song, he sat on the couch, it was evening, and Mum closed her eyes and leaned against him.

But he was sick then and he knew it, I think, he knew it long before we did. And later, at the hospital, then I tried to sing it to him. But he turned away under the duvet, just like when I stroked his arm, it hurt him, and I stopped stroking him and singing.

Now Cecilie was singing that song.

> *She showed me her room*
> *isn't it good*
> *Norwegian wood?*

Everything made sense again. In a pattern, a meaning.

And every morning I awoke before her. When the sun shone through the window, she just put her braid over her eyes and kept sleeping. While I stood on the wooden floorboards and looked at her.

'Can we take a little break?' Mikael said.

I turn around.

They are standing still.

'Already?' I say.

He nods.

'The village is just right down there,' I say.

Mia squints. She always does that when she has a headache.

'We can rest for five minutes,' I say. 'You can have some alphabet crackers.'

I lift the kids up onto a snow bank. Then I pull off my mittens and put my rucksack on the ground and rummage around inside it until I find the box of alphabet crackers, my fingers are as cold as ice, it hurts around my fingernails. I can't be bothered to find an M for both of them, I give them an R and a Q and put on my gloves again, and then I point towards the other side of the valley.

'That's called the tree line,' I say.

Mikael nods.

'That's the Great Bear,' I say. 'And now the moon is almost full, you can see that, can't you?'

But it's like they aren't paying attention. Mia looks at her cracker. Then she puts it down beside her on the snow bank.

'Eat a little,' I say. 'Then it will pass, for sure.'

She bows her head. I place a mitten under her chin, but she twists away, my mitten is cold.

'Are you worried?' I ask.

'I don't know,' she answers.

Then I look at the moon. Those shadows aren't bodies of water. It would be totally nuts to think there could be water on the moon. Nonetheless that's what they're called: Sea of Tranquillity, Sea of Serenity, Lake of Dreams. People are not very logical.

'I'm hungry,' Mikael says.

'You can have a few more crackers,' I say and shake crackers out of the box, then I find the package of painkillers in the side pocket of my rucksack and press out two tablets, and put them in Mia's mitten.

'Do we have water?' she says.

She looks at me. I shake my head. I don't have any water. She puts the tablets in her mouth and looks away and swallows. I clap my hands together and rock a bit from side to side. A few houses are glittering down in the valley.

'Isn't it nice here?' I say.

'Very,' Mikael answers.

'Do you see down there?' I say. 'Our cottage will glitter like that, too.'

Mikael kicks his heels into the snow bank.

'So,' I say. 'Now we have to move on.'

They just sit there.

'We must move on now,' I say. 'If we sit here, then we'll freeze to death.'

Then Mikael slides down off the snow bank. I pat Mia on the arm.

'Shall I carry your rucksack on my tummy?' I ask.

She nods.

'My rucksack is heavy, too,' Mikael says.

*

But the hills must be coming to an end now soon.

It's cold, I think it's getting colder, it's just like a heavy cold is sinking down towards us.

'You two are good little walkers,' I say.

But it's not true. They're not good at walking, they're city kids, they're good at changing trains and they don't reply, because they don't like it when I fib. I am out of breath. The air is so cold sliding down into my lungs.

I turn around. Mia scuffs her feet along the ground.

'Mia,' I say. 'Did the painkillers work?'

'Maybe,' she says.

We should have taken a taxi. The hill is too steep, their legs are too short. And Mia has a headache, of course she does.

'I think that's the top there,' I say.

'And then we're there,' Mikael says.

'Not quite,' I say.

I keep walking. I stare at the top. But now I can see, how something is flapping over the edge, with every step it flaps more and more, I look at the ground instead, and walk a little bit more and look up again, and see it. Yet another hilltop.

I stop. Mikael catches up with me.

'That wasn't the top,' he says.

'Wait a minute,' I say.

'But is that the top there?' he says.

'Hush,' I say. 'Just rest here for a little while.'

Mia sits, she sits right down, against the edge of the snow bank. I put my rucksack and their rucksacks on the ground. Mikael pulls off one mitten and pulls the pen out of his pocket.

'Put the mitten on,' I say.

He puts on the mitten.

'How are you feeling?' I ask.

'Fine,' Mikael says.

But Mia doesn't say anything. She sits like a small animal on the side of the road. And now the cold and the darkness sort of get inside me. Because how are we going to manage this? And now I remember all the things I don't manage, I see those kinds of signs again, it's like that evening, it was my turn to sing, I lay on my back on the couch with the guitar on my tummy and sang 'The Wolf Song', I didn't know how to accompany it, but here and there I hit notes that fit. It was late, the fire had almost gone out. Then I finished singing.

I was embarrassed. I stood up and lay a log in the fireplace.

'You should put birch on the fire with the bark facing in,' Cecilie said. 'Then it catches fire.'

I leaned over and picked up another log from the wood basket and put it in the way she said.

'No, that one is spruce,' Cecilie said.

'Oh,' I said.

'Birch is white. Don't you know that?' Cecilie said.

'No,' I answered.

'Oh,' Cecilie said. 'I thought everyone knew what birch was.'

'Not me,' I said.

'No,' Cecilie said. 'Spruce sparks, you see.'

I stood there with the log in my hand. Then I put it back in the basket. I went into the kitchen and got a glass of water.

Afterwards I went back into the living room.

'Are your feelings hurt?' she asked.

I didn't reply.

'Sorry if I said something stupid,' she said.

'That's OK,' I said.

She smiled then. I sat down on the edge of the couch.

'That song was nice,' Cecilie said. 'The one you sang before.'

'Thanks,' I said.

She was lying in the other corner of the couch. She was tired and rubbed her face.

'What kind of a song is it?' she asked.

'It's from a movie I saw with the kids,' I answered. '*Ronia, The Robber's Daughter*.'

'Ronia,' Cecilie said. 'That's not really a movie. It's a book.'

Then she drew her hair away from her face. Then she fell asleep.

But I didn't sleep. I sat on the couch and stared at her. She rolled over onto her side, all I could see was hair. And then I understood: I was going to lose her.

I looked out the window. The forest was completely silent there. But it was just like it was full of signs, the darkness between the trees, and it is the same forest here, it is the same darkness and the same feeling: I am going to lose them.

Mia stares at me from beneath the brim of her hood.

Now she's not going to give up, I can see it on her, now she will just ask and ask and ask, and I can't take that. She opens her mouth.

'Why are we here?' she asks.

'Because nobody can find us here,' I say.

'But what happens if they find us?' she asks.

'They won't,' I say.

'But if they do?' she asks.

Oh, I am too tired now. I won't manage to fib at the right time, it's because last night I lay awake, I tossed and turned beneath the duvet, and it's because I had to pretend everything was fine all day, and hide my rucksack from Mum and pay for the bus without looking the driver in the eyes, I can't take any more now, I won't manage it, it's because I'm nervous, and because I'm so tired from the rucksacks, my shoulders hurt.

'What?' I say.

'What happens then?' Mia says. 'If they find us?'

I'm too tired. I'm unable to lie.

'Then I have to move,' I say.

'Away from us?' Mia asks.

I look down at my shoes. They are no good, they are just city shoes, they are not nearly warm enough.

'But what will happen to us then?' Mia says.

And I know what she wants, she wants to be reassured. But I can't reassure her, not if I tell the truth, because they won't manage without me and I remember how it was when it was at its worst, when Dad was dead and people came and gave us big pots of food, but they were left standing cold on the cooker, and people came and gave us flowers and I clipped the cards off the bouquets and showed them to Mum, she sat on the couch and held the cards on her knee, but I saw that she didn't read them, her eyes didn't move, then she put them on the couch beside her.

But we managed.

Because I knew how to do everything.

Make pack lunches and pizza, hang the clothes out to dry. I didn't have so many feelings. But now, now I have far too many.

'Tell me,' Mia says. 'Will you have to move away from us or can we move in with you?'

'Away,' I say.

'And what if you say that you don't want to?' she asks.

'It won't help,' I say.

'But what if we say that you are going to take care of us?' she asks.

'Stop,' I say.

'But what if,' she says.

'Stop,' I say. 'It's not going to happen.'

'I just said *what if*,' Mia says.

'But you always say *what if*,' I say. 'You have to stop. You wear me out.'

'But what did you do wrong?' Mia asks.

And then I don't say anything else, I stand there, shifting my weight from side to side.

Because I know what I did wrong.

My only job is to take care of them, but I didn't manage it.

I stand there shifting my weight from side to side. I look at the moon, I have tears in my eyes. The moon sparkles and blurs into a star.

I continue walking up the hill, they can't see that I'm crying, but now they have to call out to me, because they need me, but they don't call and then more tears are rising, quick and salty, that's how I am, it doesn't take much with me, that's how I am, that's how I destroy things, and the week went by fast up here, and then it was the day before we were going home and I was nervous, because I had decided to be brave. I didn't ever usually ask her about anything, I didn't want to fuss, but then the last day came and then I'd decided to ask after all, we were sitting on towels in the heather by her old swing, it was tied to a branch, she pushed it, and it swung back and forth. The ropes were worn and light blue. So I took a breath. I had planned exactly how I would ask, how one question would lead to the next.

'Do you have any plans for the autumn break?' I said.

'The autumn break?' Cecilie said.

'Yes,' I said.

We could see out across the bog from there. The heather stuck to our thighs, the towel was worn thin.

'I thought that maybe we could come here again,' I said.

'But I don't know if I'll have a break,' she said.

I turned and looked at her.

'I guess you'll have a break if I do,' I said.

'But I don't know if they have the same system in England,' she said.

That's how she said it. She just looked straight out across the bog and said it like that.

And afterwards when I walked away through the trees and the pine needles prickled the soles of my feet and she came after me and held me tight, then she said that she was sure she had told me before, completely sure, that she'd applied, been accepted, and received a grant and everything. But she hadn't. I'm not deaf. I have a brain.

'But I applied in January,' she said. 'I applied long before we got to know each other.'

And I didn't say it, but I thought: How could she leave me when I could never leave her. I didn't say it, but she understood what I was thinking anyway, because that was the question she answered.

'We are two different people, after all,' she said.

We stood between the tree trunks and her eyes were too clear, they stared straight into mine and it hurt me, my thoughts and my heart were in pain, her freckles were light brown and her braid was loose and I understood what she wanted: to get away from me.

Then she held me and she said she would write a lot of letters and send a lot of photographs, but my body stiffened, I didn't like her talking into my ear any more, I didn't like it that she held me close, and she did send letters, not a lot, but two. It was autumn then. My hands were white when I opened the letter box. And the letters were thick, with small messages written on the envelopes, but I didn't read them, I didn't open them, I threw them straight into the recycling bin. And after I had thrown out two, I didn't receive any more. One envelope was white and one was blue.

I turn around.

Mikael sticks his pen into the snow bank. I look up at the sky. And there is Venus.

It's Venus.

And I remember. Dad stood behind me and pointed out the planets. I remember he lifted my ponytail and stroked my neck and said *you're a clever one, you are, my little girl.*

It's the truth. The way I was, how I really am.

I manage to figure things out.

I've always managed it, I've always been able to see how things are put together, where on the shoelace I'm supposed to loosen the knot, where in Mia's hair I should start combing, I turn the bicycle upside down and stare at the gears until I understand it, I find the right little screwdriver to fix it with.

Now I look at the kids and think. And understand.

We're not going to be able to walk there.

We need a ride.

But I know what happens when they put out a missing persons alert. The taxi drivers are the first people the police call.

So what shall we do?

I have to think.

I stare up at the sky. Venus is not a star, it's a planet. It's so wrong all the things everyone thinks. People don't think logically, it is many billion miles closer than the closest star.

I close my eyes.

It was Venus. Full of embers and carbon dioxide, like the fireplace, *all heat is the same heat*, my father said.

We need a ride.

We have to hitchhike.

I open my eyes. I walk down to the kids.

'We'll get a ride,' I say.

'Will we?' Mikael says.

'Yes,' I say. 'Isn't that good?'

'Very,' Mikael says.

'So you can just sit down and rest a little now,' I say. 'Like Mia's doing.'

Mikael sits down. Mia is resting her forehead against her knees.

Then I explain to them that in the car they mustn't say a word. Mustn't say their names. Mustn't say where we're going.

'And Mia,' I say. 'You have to keep your hood on the whole time.'

Mia doesn't say anything.

'And if there's somebody asking a lot of questions, then we just get out of the car,' I say.

'A car is coming down there,' Mikael says.

He's right about that, two yellow headlights are approaching. They disappear behind a bend, then they reappear, headed towards us, I can hear the engine now. Mia lifts her head.

'Can't we get a ride with them?' she says.

'We can't get into a car with just anybody,' I say.

'But can't we ride in that one?' she asks.

'Maybe,' I say.

I walk a few steps out into the road.

'First I have to check who's driving it,' I say.

The lights draw closer, but it's impossible to see inside, of course, I can't see who it is, of course, but what shall I do?

I stick out my thumb and then walk a few steps as the headlights grow larger and larger. It's just an optical illusion, but everything is light, actually, and all lights are the same light, that's what my father said.

*

It's a woman.

She has rolled down the window, she's looking at me. I cross the road and walk over to the car. It smells of pizza. She looks at the kids and back at me.

'Are you hitchhiking?' she asks.

I nod. My hat slips down my forehead. She has pretty hair, blonde, it hangs around her face like feathers.

'Where are you going then?' she asks.

'Just up the hill here,' I say.

She looks at the kids again. There is calm music playing on her car radio.

'Then you're standing on the wrong side of the road,' she says. 'But come on, get in.'

She has nice eyebrows, high and dark. Her sweater is beige. There is a pizza box on the passenger's seat. But her eyes are light blue, husky eyes, wolf eyes.

I walk back to the kids and pick up the rucksacks and tell them to come.

I put the rucksacks in the boot, I open the back door. The lady turns around and looks at Mikael.

'You can sit in the child seat,' she says. 'You're about four years old, maybe?'

He doesn't answer, he's a good boy. She has moved the pizza box, now it's in the back.

Then I walk around the car with Mia and open the door for her. I sit in the front seat and close the door.

She turns down the volume on the radio.

'Where is it you said you're going?' she asks.

'I'll just let you know when we want to get out,' I reply.

I take off my hat. She looks at me. I know she's thinking that I'm strange. I tuck my hair behind my ears, I know she's trying to find out what kind of girl I am.

She starts driving.

'Are you going to stay at a cottage?' she asks.

'Mm,' I say.

She looks in the rear-view mirror. I glance behind me and see what she sees. Mia, she's wearing her hood, she's leaning towards the window. And Mikael, he's sitting and staring at his pen. His skin is so dark. I know she gets that we have three different fathers.

'Yes, we've had a lot of snow,' she says.

I nod.

'And there's been no thaw this winter,' she says. 'So breaking trail is heavy going now.'

'Yes,' I say.

'But maybe you're not all that interested in cross-country skiing?' she says.

I shake my head.

'I just assumed,' she says. 'Most of the visitors come here to go skiing.'

This is exactly the kind of conversation that I am incapable of having.

You're listening to NRK P2, a voice says, then there's another sound and somebody starts talking. It's the news. She reaches out a hand and switches off the radio and glances at me.

'I was thinking about the kids,' she says.

I don't understand what she means.

'I don't know if they're usually allowed to listen to the news?' she says. 'My daughter isn't allowed.'

'No,' I say. 'Thank you.'

She looks at the road again, it curves, every metre that I manage to remain in the car is good, every metre is one metre less for the kids to walk. I just have to manage to behave normally.

'So you're travelling alone?' she asks.

I nod. I look out the window. There's a kind of drop-off on my side, there must be a lake down there, at the other end of the lake is a waterfall, it's frozen, it's pretty. I look back at the dashboard.

It's -13 °C.

'Did you take the bus from Oslo then?' she asks.

'Hmm?' I say.

'Now, dear,' she says and then she smiles.

And now I can feel it. She does something. She touches me. And my whole body stiffens. She takes my hand and I hate it. I hate the skin of strangers, I hate that they are so lukewarm, just like me, it gives me a disgusting feeling all through my body. She pats my hand.

'You seem so out of sorts,' she says. 'Did something happen?'

Then I unfasten my seatbelt.

'Can you stop?' I say. 'I think we'd rather walk after all.'

'What?' she says.

'Can you stop?' I say.

'I can't stop right here,' she says.

I lean towards her and stare at her face. So my charisma will have its effect.

'Why not?' I ask.

'Because we're in a turn,' she says, but I know it's a lie, I know she wants to catch us, and we can't get caught now.

I put my hand on the emergency brake.

She glances down. I start to pull the brake, it makes a clicking sound.

Then she twists the steering wheel to one side. She pushes a button with a triangle on it and everything starts blinking.

'Go ahead,' she says. 'Now you can get out.'

I turn towards the back seat.

'Come on,' I say.

Mikael unfastens his seatbelt and crawls out of the car. I open my door, it doesn't open all the way, we're too close to the snow bank. I wriggle my way out and backwards and open Mia's door. I lean inside and undo her seatbelt. But she won't move out of the seat.

'Can you take her out so I can drive,' the woman says. 'Stopping here is dangerous.'

'Come on now, Mia,' I say.

'Don't say that,' Mia says.

'What?' I say.

'That's not my name,' Mia says and she starts shaking her head. She leans towards me, she whispers.

'I'm too tired,' she whispers.

The lights blink. I put my hands around Mia's hood.

What shall I do now?

If she refuses to walk, then we'll end up standing here until somebody comes to pick us up. And I know who picks up people like us.

Now I have to think clearly.

The worst thing or the second worst thing. What will most certainly go wrong or the other thing.

I stand up and close the back door and walk to the front door now. I bend over and look the woman in the eyes. Cecilie said it, *you have to look people in the eyes if you want them to trust you.*

'Can we have a ride after all?' I ask. 'My sister isn't well.'

She draws a breath. I see that she's thinking, she looks at Mia, she looks out the window, she looks at me.

'Of course,' she answers. 'Get in.'

*

Mia is leaning against the door. Her hood is off. Her hair is visible.

But it's my fault that we'll be remembered now. I am bloody incapable of having an ordinary conversation, but that's because, that's because we always have something to hide. *What are you doing for your summer holiday?* people ask, *where does your father live*, but we can't really answer, we really have to lie about everything.

She drives 60 kilometres an hour. It's fourteen below zero. A small arrow is blinking beside the speedometer. I don't know what it means, she has such a nice car. And she gave us a ride.

'Excuse my rudeness,' I say.

She looks straight in front of her.

'That's fine,' she says.

'We're not used to people asking us about so many things,' I say.

'No,' she says. 'I won't ask you anything else.'

Then there aren't any streetlights any longer. The darkness comes from all sides. She switches on the brights. Her hair is very clean, very blonde and fine. I have to talk about the kinds of things people talk about.

There is a car approaching us, she moves her hand and switches on the dimmer.

'What do you work with? I ask.

'Product design,' she answers.

The car passes. She puts on the brights again. I nod.

'What do you design?' I say.

'Right now I'm working on a fork,' she says.

'A fork?' I say.

'Yes,' she says.

'Aren't there sort of enough forks already?' I ask.

'Yes,' she answers.

Then she smiles. She's different when she smiles, I look at her and have to smile, too.

'Maybe that was a strange way to put it,' I said.

'Yes, it was,' she says. 'But you're absolutely right.'

Then she laughs.

*

She puts on the brakes and I look up. The headlights fall on a sign, there is a fork in the road in front of us.

'What is it?' I say.

'Here we have to choose, she says. 'Are you going to the cottage district or further in?'

'There,' I say and point to the left.

'The cottage district,' she says.

She turns in the direction I am pointing, the road narrows, I know where I am now, we drive up through the birch forest, then we slip over the ridge and there it opens up, down there is Aurtjern, closer and closer and larger and larger, the moon shines on the snow, we reach the turnaround, there's the boom barrier and that's where the boat was, we sat there. She stops by the letter box rack.

'We're going in there,' I say.

I point.

'That's a private entrance,' she says.

'Yes?' I say.

'I don't have a cottage here,' she says.

'No?' I say.

She looks at me.

'Yes, only the cottage owners have keys,' she says. 'To the boom barrier.'

I nod.

'Of course,' I say. 'That wasn't what I meant.'

Then I turn towards the kids.

'We're here,' I say.

But we're not here.

'Anyway, it hasn't been ploughed from the looks of it,' the woman says.

I lean forward. And now I see what she sees. Behind the boom barrier the snow is much deeper.

'Oh,' I say.

'What is it?' Mikael says.

'Nothing,' I say. 'When will it be ploughed?'

'I don't know,' she says. 'Maybe at the weekend.'

'What day is it today?' I ask.

'Tuesday,' she replies.

Mikael looks at us, back and forth.

'Shall I drive you somewhere else?' she asks.

'No,' I answer. 'This is where we we're going.'

I put on my hat and get out.

The kids follow. I lift the rucksacks out of the boot. I give Mikael his rucksack. I put Mia's rucksack on in front and my own rucksack on my back.

'Hey, listen,' the woman says. 'Do you want this?'

She has opened the door and is holding out the pizza box.

'No, thank you,' I say. 'Daddy will pick us up here in a little while.'

She doesn't answer. I smile at her.

'Thank you for the ride,' I say.

'My pleasure,' she says.

Then I turn away, I take the kids by their hands. We walk towards the boom barrier. I hear the sound of her car as she drives away.

*

Then it's quiet.

What do we do now?

What do we do now, now that we're all alone.

'Is there a wolf here?' Mikael says.

I turn my head. Her car is gone. There is something on the ground. It's the pizza box.

'Is there?' Mikael says.

'What?' I say.

I've thought of everything. The bus and the money, the key on the birdfeeder. I bought tins of food, I found warm clothes and matches and packed everything in plastic bags, I hid the bags between the bins, then I picked up Mia, then I picked up Mikael, then we took the bus, but now we're here.

Now we're just standing here.

I forgot all about the boom barrier.

And I put my hand on the emergency brake, my mind failed me, it's my fault that we'll be remembered now. Mia sits down on the ground. Mikael takes the pen out of his pocket and draws something in the air with it, something I can't make out. And there's Aurtjern and we always went swimming there, an old boat was lying there upside down and I remember the first day. I lay on my stomach on top of the boat and dried off in the late afternoon sun and she lay on her back on a towel and said *I don't understand why we live in the city, Rebekka. What are we doing there?*

I pushed myself up off the boat. I picked small triangular paint flakes off my tummy.

'We should live here,' she said.

'Yes,' I said.

But a few days later, it was only a few days later, then we walked back here and the boat was still there, but everything was different. We had rucksacks on our backs but we didn't talk to each other any longer and the taxi was waiting here and I hated every single step, but I had to go, I had to get in and look out the window, at the mountains and everything. It was the same driver, but now he didn't say anything and we had to take the bus home and I had to look at her and say goodbye and walk through the city and unlock the door and at home everything was the same as before. I entered the flat, it smelt the same, but she was leaving.

And then she left.

She went to England.

And what about me. I had apparently not changed one bit. Everything just trickled away, the cottage and the French and the Toyen swimming pool at night and my plans, the office at the university, it was like it no longer existed. But it was still the summer holiday and I had nothing to do. So I just did whatever. I just walked around in the summer in Oslo and did whatever, I didn't care any longer. It's true what they wrote, *acts out and has no sense of boundaries*, and when the kids fell asleep, I put eyeliner around my eyes and the fake ID in my pocket and went out, to the pub, I opened the door and the women looked at me. They leaned towards one another and whispered, but I didn't care, I went to the bar, I know what they were talking about, about who I was, the daughter of my mum. And night came and I argued with people or went home with people from there, weekend fathers and drunks and refugees, in the sitting rooms their kids' play mats were lying on the floor, pictures of other girlfriends were hanging on the refrigerators. It helped me at night.

And when I went home at first light, everything was a little bit better. And when I went to bed then, I slept deeply and it felt good. But when school started again, I couldn't get up in the morning.

None of us could.

Because that's how we are, one for all. I awoke in the morning from the yellow light in the room, far too warm, far too late and far too much sunlight. The kids' rucksacks were in the hallway and I saw the queue in front of the bakery when I ran to school, because it came undone for us, and in the afternoons I was angry. I set the frying pan down hard on the table and everyone became afraid of me. Mum jumped every time a door opened or closed and Mikael had nightmares about a cat, because that's how we are, all for one, and if I tried to go to bed early, I woke up in the middle of the night and my heart was pounding and I just had to go out, I felt so restless, an itchiness in my body and I was useless at school, so the teachers had to talk with me.

And some of them were strict and took me into their offices and pointed out my absences and said:

And what this means is that if you are absent one more day, you will have an incomplete, and some were nice and tried to understand, they tilted their heads to one side and said *you made such good progress last spring, if you get a doctor's note, the absence can be deleted.*

But I couldn't get a doctor's note. What would I tell the doctor? That I get sick from not having friends, I get sick from sleeping with strangers, I get sick and tired and I have nobody to talk with, do you have any medicine for this?

'Are there?' Mikael asks.

'Answer him,' Mia says. 'He's asking if there are wolves here.'

I look down. They look up.

'There aren't any wolves in Norway,' I say.

Then I shake myself, I shake my entire body and look up at Venus and then I say: 'Now we'll eat a little pizza. And then we'll walk the last stretch.'

*

But I didn't know that snow could be like this. I am sweating, I take off my hat, but then it's freezing cold, I pull the hat on again. I move one leg at a time. I didn't know that snow could be like this, impossible to walk through, like a swimming pool or a nightmare.

Just over this way and to the right. We can do this.

I stop.

I have to think clearly.

We can't bring the rucksacks with us.

'Take off your rucksack,' I say.

Mikael pulls off the rucksack.

I remove Mia's rucksack and my rucksack. They sink into the snow, they almost disappear.

'Are we going to come and get them afterwards?' Mikael asks.

I nod. Then I turn around and keep ploughing through the snow. We have to get there. One step at a time. I have to be smart. And strong. Not weak and dumb. But it's dangerous, because I can get that way, weak and dumb, I became that way, I was supposed to take a make-up test, *one final chance in French*, the counsellor had arranged it, she said that according to my records I'd missed far too many classes, but if I passed the test, I could pass anyway, *absolutely the last chance*, she'd said. And I tried then, to pull myself together. It was November, the leaves lay dark and slippery on the sidewalks and I tried to pull myself together. I didn't go to the pub, I got up when the alarm went off and pulled the kids through the streets and dropped them off in the dark. I stared up at the blackboard, but my mind was fuzzy, I was unable to remember, because Mikael, he didn't sleep at night, he dreamt about that cat, it changed colours in his dream and opened its mouth towards him and then he woke up and cried. I studied in the sitting room with earplugs in my ears, but I could hear through them and it was like I was unable to learn anything when he was crying. And then Mia woke up too and started becoming strange. She got a headache and her teacher sent her to the school nurse and she came home with a note that said she needed to be checked for child migraines, could somebody take her to such and such a centre.

But I tried to think clearly. Then I decided that I didn't want Mikael to take a nap at day care, so I told the staff and they agreed with me.

But he tricked them.

He slept in the lavatory. He slept on the round log by the sandbox, on his tummy, with a spade in his hand. He was sleeping on the swing when I arrived. He pretended to be swinging but he was sleeping, with his head against the chain.

And then there was the French test. It was supposed to be on Friday and then it was Thursday and I had barely studied at all. The afternoon came and I ran towards the day-care centre in the darkness, I slipped between parked cars, I was too late because I'd fallen asleep at the kitchen table while I was trying to cram, I opened the chain latch on the gate and ran past the sandboxes and pulled open the door and Mikael was lying there in his leggings, on the bench in the changing room, .

It was my fault. I was too late. The woman who had the late shift was sweeping up the floor.

But it was my last chance and the test had become like a symbol and I was so stressed and exhausted from this waking up business of his, I shook Mikael, but he didn't wake up so I sat down on the bench that is too narrow for your bum. I hauled him onto my lap and pulled on his trousers, but he didn't wake up.

My hands were as cold as ice, I had forgotten my mittens. Mikael's body hung heavily across my legs and the woman who had the late shift came and stood there with her coat on and holding a bunch of keys in her hand, she wanted to leave. But she looked at me. She smiled.

I remember what she said.

'Tough days,' she said.

Her coat was long and brown, it looked soft.

'Yes,' I said. I struggled with Mikael's boots, his legs were limp and my hands didn't work, they were frozen, it was impossible to get his boots on.

So I gave up. I banged my head against the wall behind me. It didn't hurt, because there were clothes hanging in the way, I banged it once more, harder, I wanted it to hurt.

Then the woman put the bunch of keys on the bench and squatted down.

She took hold of Mikael's leg and pushed on his boot. His head fell to one side. She pushed on the other boot. Then she looked up at me, outside the window it was black, it was probably well after five, we probably should have been thrown out a long time ago.

'Are you doing all right these days?' she asked.

I drew a breath.

I should have just nodded.

Or thought about it. I should have just answered *what do you mean*. Or. I should have just got up and left.

But then I shook my head.

'No?' she said.

She supported herself with one hand on the bench. Her coat spread like a dark shadow across the floor. And then I could have pulled myself together.

But I failed to pull myself together.

'No,' I said.

And then she asked some more and I answered her questions. You're not supposed to do that, but I was weak then, because of Cecilie and the French test and that cat and Mum who didn't call work back and Mia who had to have a doctor's exam, because of everything, it was too much. But I didn't say that. I just said *I can't get my homework done. I don't have time. And I know I'm supposed to pick him up by 4.45 actually, but I just can't make it.*

'I understand,' she said. 'Don't give it another thought.'

All the while Mikael continued sleeping and then she got coffee for us. She took off her coat and laid it over Mikael and called her husband and said she would be a little late.

And then she asked about Mia's father. I shook my head. And she asked about Mikael's father and I said *he's in Morocco getting married.*

'And your father,' she said. 'He's no longer alive?' She just said it like that.

'No,' I said.

'So all this gets to be too much for you,' she said. I nodded.

I held my hands around the cup, my fingers thawed out. Then she said that it wasn't supposed to be like this.

'You have to be able to do your homework,' she said.

'Yes,' I said.

She smiled. And reached out her hand and patted me on the cheek and said: 'Well, we're going to straighten this out, Rebekka. You're not supposed to live like this.'

'No,' I said.

And she said *you are so clever, the kids are so lovely, we are so fond of all of you.* And me, I just said yes.

'Yes,' I said.

'But now I'm going to give you some money,' she said. 'And then I will call a taxi to drive you home.'

She leaned over her purse and found her wallet and took out 300 kroner.

'Thank you,' I said.

She went into her office and called. I sat on the bench with Mikael. Then she was standing in front of us again and said: 'And when you get home, I suggest that you just let him sleep. Just put him to bed with his clothes on and if you're lucky, he'll sleep through the night. Then you can study.'

She seemed to know everything.

She lifted her cup.

And I sat there with three 100-kroner notes in my hand, she walked towards the kitchen, I stood up and followed behind her, it was dark there, we put the cups in the sink and she turned towards me and said *do you feel a little better now, are you a bit calmer now*?

I nodded.

She went out into the hallway and turned off the lights and turned on the alarm and lifted Mikael into her arms, I followed them out into the darkness and at the gate the taxi driver stood smoking in front of his car. She laid Mikael on the backseat, she said to the driver: 'Let's forget about the seatbelt and you just drive safely' and the driver nodded and dropped the cigarette butt on the ground, then we drove home in the dark and everything went as she'd said. There were 150 kroner left over and I carried Mikael inside and laid him right in his bed.

That night they both slept.

And in that silence I crammed.

The window was shiny and outside everything was black, my thoughts were so clear, like there was room in my head again. I understood everything again, the differences and the similarities, subjunctive and indicative, the logic was inside me again and then it was three o'clock and I knew the entire syllabus, I lay down on the bed and slept, just a few hours, but so well, so deeply.

And the next day I passed the test. And the same day she called children's services.

She did.

But I'm not there now, in the corridors with linoleum on the floor, in the bloody conference rooms. Here is where I am and the snow is clean and it's quiet and soon we will be at the cottage, nobody can see us here and I'm not sitting in a conference room with psychologists and forms, *how often do you have uncontrolled outbursts of rage, how often in the past week have you felt that you want to die.* Oh, I couldn't stand any of it, and there are pictures of sunflowers on the walls and the conference tables are so clean and shiny and the women are so confident and I answer everything wrong and become furious and stand up and hit the wall and see the women jump and then we have to have a network meeting and I didn't manage to pull myself together then either and I cried because nobody understood and I spoke loudly because nobody understood and I noticed how I smelt of sweat and Mum and Morten and Mehmet looked at me. And I stood up and crumpled up the papers and afterwards we stood in the car park and Mum's hair blew in all directions and Morten said *you sure handled that badly, Rebekka,* and Mehmet nodded, Mehmet, the one who loses it if someone parks too close to his car.

But I shouldn't have punched the wall. I shouldn't have crumpled up papers. I know that and I shouldn't have hidden afterwards, I shouldn't have wandered around in the Botanical Gardens and thought that if only I wandered long enough, everything will be fine, then they would forget about me, I shouldn't have let Mum go alone to meetings, I should have kept combing my hair, I should have thought logically, I was the one who made mistakes. Because they trick you and trick you and trick you, further and further into the labyrinth and finally you are standing there and can't move and then you receive mail, then you receive a letter, *the girl's behaviour has become too difficult for the mother to handle*, then you must sit on the bed and open such letters with your own hands and read what they write, *the mother gives her consent for voluntary placement, it is the assessment of child care services that placement in an institution a short distance away from Oslo would be in the girl's best interest.*

And they don't understand what will happen then.

They don't understand who I am.

I am the one who takes care of them.

'Look at Mia,' Mikael says.

I turn around.

'But where is she?' I ask.

Mikael raises his arm.

'She's standing there,' he says.

Far behind us. Like a small tree between the trees.

'Come on,' I say.

Mikael follows behind me, we stagger down our own path, but what's wrong with her, why is she standing there like that. I stop in front of her.

'What is it?' I ask.

She lies on her back in the snow.

'Can't you take any more?' I ask.

She doesn't reply.

'Because of your head?' I ask. 'Do you want another painkiller? Shall I go get you one?'

But she doesn't answer. She just lies there. Her braid has come undone, the elastic is gone and strands of hair are lying across her face, like brooks or clay or blood. Something I don't want to see. Then she turns her head to one side. She retches. Nothing comes out, but she retches again, she gets like this, it's not serious, it's just the migraines. Her body jerks. Then she stops.

'Shall I carry you?' I ask.

She nods.

'Fine,' I say. 'Get on my back.'

I crouch down in front of her. She puts her arms around my neck, I take hold of her under her bum, she's so heavy when she's limp, but I stand up, I hold her around her thighs, I keep going.

Just over this way and to the right.

But now I sort of don't understand where the roads are, is that a road or is it a brook or a path or what?

'I'm really cold,' Mikael says.

And so he is, we are moving very slowly now, I sink even deeper because of Mia.

'I know,' I say. 'But we're almost there now.'

Because we have to be.

I have to stay sensible. That's the only way to get things to work out just fine.

I've thought it all through. And I packed the way Cecilie told me to a long time ago, matches, painkillers and toilet paper, I remembered everything, I remembered the bus schedule and the church and the bus stop, all of that was stored in my mind, how to turn on the gas, how to open the damper and stack kindling in the fireplace.

We have to get there.

To the fireplace and the gas flame. The couch I can lay Mia on. The sheepskins and wool blankets and how I will wrap her up in them, the broth I will cook, how Mikael will stretch his fingers towards the fireplace.

And I remember what my father said: *All heat is the same heat; all heat is a tiny big bang.*

I turn my head and say to Mikael: 'Think about a fire.'

'Yes,' he says.

I nudge Mia's body up higher. I move one leg after the other.

'Think about the sun,' I say.

'Yes,' Mikael says.

Everything is sliding so oddly. Everything is so heavy, I get dizzy. I just have to stand still for a bit.

'What else?' Mikael says.

And I look up at the sky, I look up at the stars and far, far inside my head, but I can't come up with anything else that is warm.

'Are we there?' Mikael asks.

I shake my head.

And then I drop Mia. Her arms slip from around my neck.

I turn around. She's just lying there, in the snow, with her eyes closed.

I am the kind who manages things. *My guardian angel*, Mum said. *You seem so wise*, Cecilie said.

'Mia?' I say. 'You have to wake up. You have to hang on.'

'Yes,' she says.

But she can't manage it. I can see that.

If only I had a sled or skis. Something to pull her on.

But I don't. And I can't turn around. And I can't keep going. But I can't stay here. What's logical then?

She has frost on her eyelashes.

'Are you cold?' I say.

'Hot,' she whispers.

But that can't be right. I take off my jacket and place it over her.

All heat is a tiny Big Bang, my father said. *You can be whatever you want*, Cecilie said. We picked heather and put it in our hair. We looked like somebody from another time. And I knew everything then, when she just looked at me, but now, now somebody should have given me advice, because now I don't know anything, now I should have had a god to pray to, *it's the laws of nature that people have confused with God*, my father said, so I look up into the sky, an airplane is blinking its lights, but an aeroplane can't help us, and I look at the forest, but the forest can't help us, and I look at the road we have followed, but a road can't help us.

Then I see it. The trees are moving. I blink hard and look again. They are still moving. Something is released from the darkness. Something is coming towards us and I start breathing, rapidly, I bend over and lift up Mia, I lift her into my arms, I call out to Mikael, *run*, and my voice is deep and strange and he tries to run but the snow is up to his tummy. Mia hangs from my arms and this is not running, because everything is just dragging, but there was something there, something black, if they catch me everything will be ruined, I hear something behind us and I run but I'm not running, my legs won't move forward and I feel something, there is someone who takes hold of me.

There is someone holding my arm.

I stop and look up and there's the Great Bear and it's always so slanted and there's the moon and it's always so full and now everything's ruined.

I turn around.

I look down.

A pink sled.

I look up.

It's her. Those eyes.

'It's just me,' she says.

I don't answer.

'Come with me now,' she says.

I shake my head.

'You can see that this won't work,' she says and turns her back to me.

What is happening now?

This isn't me, I am never like this.

But I just stand there with my arms hanging down and look at her. She bends over and lifts Mia onto the sled. Then she takes the rope in one hand and Mikael's hand in the other. She says something to him and points at our path. She glances at me again. Then she starts walking.

She just walks in our crooked path with Mikael in front of her. And Mehmet would have hit her now, and me too, I should have hit her, I should have found something hard and heavy. But I don't.

I follow behind them. Because my will is gone.

I walk here, between the trees. I pick up my jacket.

The sled sinks and gets stuck and tips up and down. It's too wide for the path.

The woman turns around.

'Can you push?' she says.

I walk up to the sled.

I bend over and do what she asks.

*

We drive. The car swings through the birch forest.

And I just swing with the car, from side to side. She looks straight ahead. It's so hot. I put my hands in front of the fan, I grow faint, it's too lovely, I let myself be fooled, the heat creeps into my body. I turn towards the backseat. And I know what I should be: hard. And I know what I should think about: the future. But I can't bear to do so now, I just want to look at the kids, Mia doesn't have that wrinkle any more, she's sitting in the middle, she's leaning her head against the child seat. Mikael turns his pen upside down, he shakes it, then he shows it to her.

'It's frozen,' she says. 'Do you see, it's ice.'

'Oh,' Mikael says.

'But you just have to heat it up,' Mia says. 'Give it here.'

They don't look at me. But I watch them, those faces, those bodies, I am always watching them, I will do that my whole life.

Then they lean towards each other and fold their hands around the pen.

I turn around again to face front.

'Do you understand what I'm doing?' I say.

But she doesn't hear me, when I ask my voice is too soft. I put my hand on her arm.

'Do you understand what I'm doing?' I say.

She nods.

'You're trying to take care of them,' she says.

'Are you planning to call someone?' I ask.

She glances at me and then back at the road.

'No,' she answers.

Then she shakes her head.

'No,' she says again. 'I hadn't planned on doing that.'